The
ACCIDENTAL
SCOUNDREL

Andrew Chapman

Also by this author

Fiction

Tripping the Night Fantastic

Non-Fiction

Last Tuesday's Shopping List[1]

---

[1] Not actually a book. Ahem…

Disclaimer

As a result of lazy research the descriptions of the Whyte and Mackay distillery are entirely made up and so any attempt to carry out the heist described within these pages would be completely idiotic and utterly fruitless.

For Kassidy

Chapter One

Sometimes you have to stop and look at yourself. You have to grab yourself firmly by the shoulders and ask, "Why? Why is this happening? You are a responsible adult, in charge of your own life, so how on earth did you get yourself into this mess?"

Unfortunately such introspection requires time to ponder. At the moment in question I didn't even have time to flush. There I was, standing at the toilet with my pyjamas around my ankles, when in walks a man with the intent to do harm. It's a great bother, being killed. It really is. It's frustrating. Imagine it. There I was, happily urinating away in the dead of night, when suddenly a man begins a full and unwarranted attack. I mean really, there must be better things an assailant could be getting on with. Yoga, embroidery, sleeping, amateur dramatics, filling their own car with exhaust fumes, anything that doesn't involve the harming of me.

Perhaps I'm somehow to blame. Who knows? Either way, adjustments to my situation clearly needed to be made. Being drowned in a toilet is not something I take pleasure in. And it is certainly not the way I wish to uncoil my mortal spring.

In the throes of death the automatic instincts of self-preservation set forth a plan of retaliation. My limbs reacted accordingly on my behalf and my brain, having made the necessary arrangements, sent a message to my lower left limb and had my foot deliver the message directly to his balls. CLOMP! What a satisfying sound.

His thick fingers tightened in my hair and yanked my head out of the toilet. In retrospect kicking him was actually a bad move. He slammed my head hard into the toilet bowl sending a shower of yellow water and smashed ceramics all over the bathroom floor. I had destroyed a toilet with my head, quite a boast I'm sure you'd agree. How this incredible act of violence didn't kill me is a mystery.

I lay like a molested fish on the cold wet tiles, my blood mingling freely with the toilet water. I felt something bump into the top of my head, something caught in the stream. I managed to raise my right arm to dislodge it and it floated past me and out of the room. I was being drowned in toilet water with a turd in it. Things seemed that little bit worse.

My murderer must have reattached his testicles because I could hear his feet stomp through the water toward me. I held my breath, I wasn't sure what he was about to do but holding my breath seemed like a good first step. In a second I had been pulled to my feet and smashed face-first into a mirror.

His hand was massive. It felt like my head was being cocooned by a deeply disturbed octopus. The right side of my face was squished up against the mirror causing my lips to do the kind of trout impression that can only be achieved with brutal force. I looked into my own reflection and rolled my eyes sympathetically.

I tried a new tactic; casual, if muffled, conversation. 'Can we talk about this?' I said.

He didn't answer with words but his actions carried a definite message. He pulled me away from the smashed mirror and slammed my head into the tiled wall.

This time he managed to knock me unconscious.

When I came around my surroundings had changed. I had, evidently, been maneuverer without my consent. While I peacefully wandered in the land of the unconscious, my attacker must have dragged me to another location in the house. The bathroom had been replaced with a more civilised environment. It doesn't seem fair does it? I mean, there I was, in my pyjamas and dressing gown, half damp and bloodied, while he looked like he was ready for a portrait and had the musk of cigars about him.

We were sitting facing each other in what I presumed to be his study. As I came out of my mild coma I shook my head and gave my face a good stretch. I even yawned. His study had burgundy walls and dark wood furniture. I've always wanted a study like his. We were sitting on brown leather chairs, the kind you imagine they have in posh gentlemen's clubs where aristocratic men go for a brandy after a good hunt. There was even a painting of a horse hung between two bookshelves and in front of that a very solid wooden desk with a lamp on it. We were positioned in front of the window. There was a small table between us with two place mats on it. Sadly there was nothing placed on them.

He had changed his clothes since I last saw him (Beating the crap out of me, as you will surely remember. Unless you have amnesia. In which case I would question your reasons for attempting to read a novel.) He was only wearing a dressing gown when he was thrashing me in his bathroom. Now he was dressed like a moustachioed Victorian.

He coughed for my attention. I suppose he's earned it in a way. I made eye contact. 'I think there's been a misunderstanding.' I said. He raised his eyebrows. Thinking he meant continue I carried on. 'You see-'

He didn't mean continue. He picked up a rifle from beside his chair and shoved the dangerous end in my mouth.

'You probably think I overreacted this morning.'

He said it like he was asking a question. I'm not sure how he expected me to answer but yes, an overreaction was certainly in progress. Luckily for me the door handle went and the lunatic pulled the gun out of my mouth and hid it beside his chair.

'Not a fucking word!' he said.

'Dad, are you in here?'

The door opened a crack letting a thin shaft of light fall across the room. It was his youngest daughter, Tiffany.

'Not now sweetheart, I'm busy.'

'What happened to the bathroom?'

It was still fairly early, I could tell by her tired voice.

'Nothing, just a little accident this morning.'

'It looks like someone had a fight in there.' She spoke through the gap in the door.

'Yes, I know, one of the horses got in the house, made a real hash up of himself.'

Brilliant, blame it on a horse, just brilliant.

'Oh god, was it Sandy? Is she ok?'

'It was Baldric.'

'Oh. Have you called for a vet?'

'Yes it's all sorted. Don't let it worry you.'

'Ok, daddy. Goodnight.'

The door closed and we were alone again.

'I take it she doesn't like Baldric?' I said.

'Nobody likes that bloody horse.'

'Fair enough. Do you mind if we talk without having the gun in my mouth?'

He shifted uncomfortably. 'Do you have children, what did you say your name was?'

'Richard. And no I don't.'

'Good for you, living the bachelor life eh?'

'Yeah, well, no, not exactly, that's why I'm here actually.'

'Ah yes, let's get back to business.'

He picked his gun back up and pressed a lever on the top of it. The double barrel came loose and fell forward. I guess it's not a rifle after all but a shotgun of some sort, I don't know much about guns but I could see as well as he could that this one was loaded. He smiled, snapped it shut, and pointed it at my chest.

'Why were you snooping around my house in the dead of night? Are you a thief?'

'No.'

'What kind of thief burgles a house in their pyjamas?'

'I'm not a thief.' I should have lied and told him I'm an escaped lunatic, or something. 'It's Mr. Rochdale isn't it?' I asked, hoping it wasn't but certain it was.

'Yes.'

His voice was authoritative and resonantly colossal. Like a dangerous echo trapped in a cave.

'Well, you know your daughter?'

'Tiffany?'

'No, not Tiffany.'

'Sarah?'

'No, not her either.'

'Natalie!?'

'Bingo!' What a stupid thing to shout. He cocked the gun.

'What have you done with my Natalie!? Kidnapped her? Killed her? You've raped her haven't you!?'

You may have noticed he has a worrying knack of jumping to conclusions. I would bet money that he's hoping for the worst just so he had a reason to beat the crap out of me again.

'You know I can legally shoot you for trespassing.'

'I don't know if that's true, but I'm not trespassing.'

The door handle interrupted us again and the door flew open and banged against an antique bureau of some sort. A lamp on top of it wobbled a bit and nearly fell over. Dramatic stuff indeed.

'Dad! What are you doing?' It was Natalie. She looked around the door and noticed me.

'Hi Nat,' I said.

'Richard, what happened to your head?'

'Oh, this,' I said, pointing at the blood that was dripping from my forehead, 'I'm trying out a new look. Also, I was about to tell your dad we're getting married.'

Chapter Two

'I'm so sorry about my dad, I did tell you to wait for me to introduce you.'

Natalie had me take a shower to wash off the dry blood, and the smell of piss, and now I was sitting on the end of her bed wearing a towel while she tended to my wounds with a dozen small plasters.

'I didn't exactly walk up to him with outstretched arms and a broad smile on my face looking for a handshake and a hearty slap on the back. It was two in the morning and I needed a wee! God knows what he thought was happening when he found me sneaking into the bathroom in my PJs? Obviously I had broken in to steal the bath!'

'He does tend to overreact. Look, you don't need to worry, I had a chance to speak to him when you were in the shower and he wants you, us, to join him for dinner this evening. And he said he won't press charges for the break in.'

'But I didn't break in!'

'I know, and he knows too, it's just his way of saying sorry.'

I dropped my head into my hands. 'I think I need to get out of this house for a few hours.'

'Please don't leave, you only got here last night.'

'No, I'm not going to leave. I just need to get out for a bit. Unfortunately, if I have any intention of marrying you, I have to find a way to befriend your mental father.'

'Well, you're either brave or crazy, but I appreciate

it. Why don't you get dressed and we'll go for a walk around the grounds.'

'And possibly find a quaint local pub for a beer?'

'If you're good.'

Beer, that's what I need. Maybe even a glass of whisky. Natalie shot off to get glammed up in a pair of muddy walking boots and a thick jumper and I threw on a pair of jeans, a dark blue t-shirt and my brown loafers. My clothes seem out of place in such a stately environment. I could have done with a pipe and a monocle, maybe even a top hat.

I met Natalie outside by the car. I tried to urge her to let us drive off and find that pub but she insisted on showing me around the grounds first. This is after all where she grew up and, *don't I want to see the annex her and her sister used to play in, or the pond they used to pretend to fish in*. I couldn't care less. I wonder if she wants to see the bins around the back of Onestop that me and my friends used to hide in and pretend were a secret bunker? Having said that I am fairly interested in seeing the stables. I want to know why no one likes Baldric.

The grounds were pretty nice. My garden when I was a kid was about the size of a small grave and had a garden gnome with no head, a pond with no water, and a staggered row of paving slabs that led from the back door to the "summer house" as my dad called it, or "shed" as it was, and a very nice collection of weeds. The grounds here are of the most outstanding beauty by comparison.

Natalie looked great. Pure beauty if you ask me. Her hair was that perfect shade of autumn blonde. No makeup, perfect complexion. She was a girl who fit her surroundings perfectly, no matter where she was.

We walked through the gate and kept to a path that took us by a six car garage on the left and around past the gardener's shed to the stables. When we got there Tiffany was brushing a sandy coloured horse who I assumed to be the aforementioned "Sandy".

'Hi Tiff,' said Nat.

'Hi Nat,' said Tiff.

I smiled and nodded. She reacted to this by rushing to her feet and bringing her horse-brush to her chest in apparent shock. 'Oh my god what happened to your head?'

'I accidently smashed a toilet with it.'

'Helping dad rescue Baldric?'

She's a fucking moron. 'Yes, helping your dad with the horse.'

'He's in bad shape,' said Tiffany.

'It's not so bad, Natalie bandaged me up good and proper.'

'Not you dummy, Baldric.'

'Baldric?'

I'm sure Natalie shared my surprise but if she did she hid it well. I didn't believe Baldric had actually been hurt at all. I thought it was a ruse. A lie made up on the spot.

'Where is Baldric?' said Natalie.

'He's in his stall,' said Tiffany, leaving Sandy's side.

Natalie and I followed Tiffany to the end of the stable to the last stall (I thought Tiffany was referring to a backless chair when she said "stall" and was slightly disappointed when my hopes to see a horse on a chair were dashed. A stall is what I would call a horse bedroom. You probably knew that.) Tiffany lifted the hinged piece of wood that kept it shut and opened the gate. Baldric was lying in a pile of bloodied hay with cuts and scratches all over his body.

'What happened to that horse?!' I shouted.

I could tell Baldric was in a bad way, I shouted pretty loudly and he didn't even flinch. Natalie nudged me in the ribs. I guessed that Tiffany was fragile and news of her dad being psychotic is sensitive information.

'Is there a vet on the way?' I asked.

'Yes, daddy called one this morning.'

'Maybe we should re-call them just in case they've forgotten.' Or in case your dad is a liar.

Baldric, as a conversation piece, had evidently been exhausted in the eyes of Tiffany and she closed the door (or should that be gate? Or something else. I know we've already established the world of equestrian architecture is beyond my sphere of knowledge but I do like to be accurate with these things). Tiffany turned her attention back to me.

'So, Nat, are you going to introduce me to your new man?'

'Fiancé,' corrected Natalie. 'This is Richard.'

'How did you manage to get hooked up and get engaged without me knowing?'

'A lot can happen without you knowing,' said Natalie. A clear dig at Tiffany's IQ that went unnoticed. So I guess it's justified.

'Well, good luck Richard, maybe you'll be the one that survives.'

'Survives? You mean people haven't in the past?'

'You already know what dad is like,' said Nat,

'He's just over protective. You'll be fine.'

'And he's only killed one of your boyfriends before,' said Tiff.

'What? He's actually killed one of your ex's?'

'Not on purpose.'

'It was a hunting accident.'

'Yeah, I'm sure it was. Look what he did to that horse!'

'It's going to be fine, once you get to know him you'll see he couldn't be a more loving man.'

'You are a liar.' I've never said that before. *You are a liar*. It's a very definite statement.

'Don't call me a liar.'

'Did it not occur to you to warn me about your mentally unhinged father before I stumbled sleepily into his death trap?'

'Everything seems worse than it is. At dinner you'll see. It's just been a big misunderstanding. He's already apologised for this morning and I know he wants to make it up to you. He wants to make a point of it after accidentally killing the last guy I brought around.'

'I'm not psychic, so I can't tell you how I know this, but you have to believe me when I say, your dad murdered your ex. It was not a hunting accident.'

'It was.'

I folded my arms and shook my head. I despaired. I worried. My eyes settled again on Baldric. 'You do realise he must have snuck out here after he knocked me out and attacked Baldric just so he had an excuse for why the bathroom was trashed. Do the words "premeditated" and "alibi" spring to mind?'

'He was confused.'

Tiffany must have been listening to our

conversation with some considerable perplexity.

'What are you two talking about? Dad didn't beat up Baldric.'

'No you're right, of course he didn't,' said Natalie.

'Ok,' said Tiff, like a perky obedient idiot. She smiled and walked back down the stables to finish brushing Sandy. Natalie and I decided the pub might be a good idea after all.

Chapter Three

The atmosphere in the pub was thick and welcoming. Loud and rambunctious. Not so much that you felt like a kitten in a Korean dog kennel, more like a chimp in a gorillas loving embrace. On the crudely plastered white walls were paintings of boats and black and white photos of famous writers. Behind an oak wood bar was a well-dressed barman and an over-stimulated barmaid. They had a simple choice of drinks; four types of whisky, three lagers, two ales, and two wines; red or white. Over by the fireplace a hound was sleeping.

The house ale tasted like old wet road kill that had been rung out into a toilet and left to ferment in there for a good decade or so, occasionally being enriched by tramps with bladder infections. Badger would be my best guess at the variety of road kill. I quietly poured it into a potted plant, which instantly shrivelled up and died, and ordered a glass of Tullamor Dew Irish whisky instead. The whisky tasted good, like a Werther's Original that had been left in my granddads pocket for a few years and then dissolved into a bottle of rubbing alcohol. Just how I like it.

Natalie sat next to me on the mandatory torn bar stool that's been fixed with grey gaffer tape, and ordered a white wine. I let the whisky warm my belly and smiled. Rochdale suddenly seemed insignificant.

'Who's this then?' said the barman.

'Richard,' I said, leaning in front of Natalie.

'He's staying with me for a few days to get to know

my dad.'

'Good luck with that mate.'

'Thanks.'

'What happened to you head?'

'Swimming accident,' I said, wondering how often I was going to get asked.

He nodded and tutted like he knew just what I meant. I liked this guy.

'Have you met our great master yet?'

'Great master?'

'He's being sarcastic,' said Nat.

'Yes I have. I helped him with a horse.'

'First impressions?'

'Please bear in mind I'm his daughter before you start saying bad things about him.'

The barman leaned in conspiratorially. 'I once saw him kick a swan in the face.'

'Shut up! You're a liar!' said Natalie, hitting him playfully, 'Why don't we talk about something else.'

'She's right,' he pointed over his shoulder at a black dome on the ceiling at the end of the bar. 'You never know when he's watching.'

I looked stunned. I know this because I caught my reflection in the mirror and almost laughed at how stupid I looked. I closed my mouth and asked the obvious question. 'He has access to your CCTV?'

'No, he has access to *his* CCTV. He owns the pub.'

'As well as the shop, church, most of the rents-'

'My balls.'

'Derek's balls,' she agreed.

Derek. I'll remember that.

The barmaid bounced over in a way that screamed infidelity, like a sex siren in a male prison, and enquired, 'Who's this?'

'Richie,' said Derek.

And already I have a nickname!

'It's just Richard,' said Natalie.

And there it goes.

Natalie must have given her the evil eye because she bounced hesitantly away again.

'What's your plan for impressing the old man?' said Derek.

'I don't know really. Just gonna take it as it goes I think. Try to not get killed.'

'That's quite a good plan. I take it you heard about the last suitor to the throne?'

'Murdered, I know.'

'My dad has never murdered anyone.'

'Sure,' said Derek the barman, leaving us to go and serve a man with an exceedingly white beard.

Natalie looked me in the eye and pouted. 'You're not really scared of him are you?'

'I'm not scared, well, I am worried. He really beat the shit out of me this morning.'

'He thought you were a burglar. Wouldn't you do the same?'

'I would rationally assess the situation first. Maybe ask a few questions.' Natalie looked down at her glass of wine but didn't say anything. 'Like, why is this thief wearing pyjamas?' She stayed silent. 'Alright, I'll wipe the slate clean. Ok? I won't even mention it again.'

She smiled and looked up, thanked me and gave me a sweet kiss on the lips. You would never get a sweet kiss where I grew up. The best you could hope for there was a kiss from a girl with only a minimal amount of

Kebab juice on her lips. I really lucked out with this one. That is if you ignore the in-law.

'Fancy some lunch?' she said.

'Yes! Feed me!'

She laughed and we finished our drinks. We left the pub to get lunch at a little sandwich shop around the corner.

There was a small scruffy boy leaning against the pub wall when we got outside. He was chewing on a candy cigarette like a gangster in a dark ally. He cocked his head and looked sideways at us. He dropped his sweet on the floor and put it out with his foot.

'Who's your friend?' he asked, looking away from us.

I actually felt intimidated until the trembling rational side of my brain got to grips with itself.

'He's none of your business,'said Natalie, walking on without slowing.

I stopped. 'I'm Richard. Who are you?'

He put his hands in his pockets and swung away from the wall and stood in front of me. Kids move like they've been created from CGI. I remember being able to climb a tree outside my house, jump on to the garage roof, shimmy up a short length of drain pipe, push a window open and be sat on the edge of my bed playing a computer game in six seconds flat. It would probably take me a fortnight to do that now.

This kid had that cocky kind of energy in spades and for some reason I had warmed to his absurd persona.

'Tommy,' said the boy. 'Nice to meet you.'

'Come on!' Natalie shouted back to me. She was almost at the sandwich shop.

'Alright, I'm coming.'

I stepped around the child and started walking after her. The boy grabbed the bottom of my jacket. I looked down at him.

'Just a friendly warning. That women you're with, she's trouble.'

He tilted his flat-cap to emphasise the seriousness of his statement and then ducked away from me and disappeared around the back of the pub.

'Richard!' shouted Nat, poking her head out of the sandwich shop.

I hurried over to join her.

'What sandwich are you having? I recommend the brie and bacon.'

'Smashing. Order up.'

Natalie ordered two bacon and brie baguettes and we sat outside on ornate patio chairs around a table with flowers etched into the white marble top. The sun was resting above the church. Natalie and I made small talk while I secretly suppressed the urge to carry on drinking.

I spotted the boy, Tommy, peering at us from inside a wheelie bin.

'What's the deal with that kid?'

Natalie looked over and Tommy ducked down. 'Don't worry about him. He's just some vagrant delinquent. Bit of a prankster.'

You always talk in short sentences when your mouth is full of French cheese. I think that's why the French are so blunt.

'He said you're trouble.'

'Maybe I am.' She winked.

I swallowed. Not for any dramatic reason, I had

simply finished chewing. 'I figured I might get your dad a bottle of whisky, or a box of cigars or something, as way of a truce. Do you think that's a good idea?'

She looked delighted. Like she finally realised that I was serious about getting on with her dad. And I was. I think. At least, I wanted to marry Nat and if that meant befriending a lunatic I was all for it.

'Yeah, that's great, there are a couple of shops farther along past the pub. There's a shop that sells penny sweets and tobacco. I wouldn't get him whisky though, he's very picky and you couldn't afford his tastes.'

'Fags and candy it is.'

'Well, you could always get the candy for me?'

'Deal. Can I get some whisky for me? My tastes are cheap.'

'You can do whatever you want.'

'Make love to this table?'

'Not that.'

'It is a nice table.'

Her smile was close to a laugh, which was fine. When we met she looked like she hadn't cracked a smile in two decades. I broke her in, opened her up. Made her smile.

We finished lunch and went to the tobacconist for the candy and cigars. I didn't buy the most expensive cigars in the shop, I went for quality, the kind of cigars a true connoisseur would give to a businessman to sweeten him up. Or so I was told. I know nothing about cigars. Thank god for the sienna-brown-coloured old lady behind the till. She knew her stuff. She looked like she bathed in nicotine.

We walked back to the manor at a slow canter. Natalie ate sweets from a small white and pink paper bag. I carried a brown bag with the cigars and a bottle of whisky. Balblair Vintage 1989. My mind was swimming in that humble liquid, making plans for the future, imagining sneaking into Rochdale's study and putting on a record, something old and bluesy, piano blues, losing myself to the drink and the tinkering of notes, plenty of black keys and changing rhythms. I shouldn't have had that drink.

Natalie headed into the house to have a bath and get ready for dinner. After all, she only had four hours to get ready. I still wasn't ready to go back into the house and face the old man so I went for another wander around the grounds.

Chapter Four

After twenty minutes or so of aimless wandering I arrived again at the stables. I thought I'd have a closer look at Baldric.

Tiffany had cleared off and the vet had come and gone. Baldric had a bandage on his front driver's-side leg (to use car terminology) and his wounds had been tended to. He was still lying down but he wasn't as out of it as he was earlier. He was chewing hay and occasionally wiggling his ears like he was trying to swat imaginary flies.

'Hi,' I said. I waited for an answer. 'Can I come in?'

He might be a horse but manners are manners. He snorted and I took it as a yes. I opened the gate and let myself in. He stopped chewing to look at me but got bored instantly and carried on. I closed the gate.

'Mind if I sit down?'

He flicked his tail. I don't know if the tail flick was a part of the imaginary fly problem he was dealing with or something else but it reminded me of a gesture a friend of mine used to make. He was a stoner. I would go over to his house after school and he'd be slumped on an old couch in a room full of smoke. I'd ask if I could sit down and he would do with his arm what the horse just did with his tail. I felt I had the experience to communicate with this horse.

I sat on the hay and tried to get comfortable. It wasn't easy. After trying a few different positions; legs crossed, lying on my side, leaning against the side of the pen, lying on my back, sitting upright with my legs outstretched, I realised there was only one place of comfort in the stable.

'Do you mind?' I asked Baldric, pointing at his belly.

Baldric looked at me and then at his belly. He snorted and carried on chewing the hay. Seemed like a yes to me. I laid back on him and drew a long breath. I let it out with a sigh. 'Have you ever thought about getting married Baldric?'

He grunted. I knew the feeling. I used to be the same.

'I know, but Natalie's different, she's not like other girls. You know what I mean?' He didn't answer. 'Do you mind if I have a drink while we talk?'

He flicked his tail. Go ahead, it seemed to suggest. I got the feeling he was trying to act all cool, like people come to him for advice all the time. I could tell he was secretly delighted to have some company.

I opened the bottle and rested my free arm on Baldric's mane. I idly ran the hair through my fingers as I pondered my life. I had a sip of whisky.

'That Rochdale's a bit of a twat though isn't he?' He let out an angry neigh and shook his head like he was trying to un-stick a memory. 'Ok, alright, we won't talk about him.'

He calmed down. Time passed easily. We shared idle chit-chat, had a few drinks, discussed love and literature and all the infinite possibilities the world had to offer. We dreamt of future conquests, and laughed about past failures. Well, more or less, as much as you can with a bruised horse.

A few hours had passed, a quarter of the whisky had vanished, and the seeds of a great friendship had been sewn. Our calm, however, was soon interrupted.

Baldric's ears suddenly pricked up. He was still. Baldric's head turned sharply and stared at a spot just beyond the wall. We were still and silent for a while, listening intently for a sound.

I heard it this time. Feet moving in foliage.

'Who's there?'

The footsteps stopped. I stood up and put the lid back on the whisky. Baldric looked at me and nodded toward the entrance. He couldn't stand but he was eager to help.

'It's ok, I'll check it out,' I said.

I opened the door to the stable and snuck to the entrance of the barn. Right beside me on the floor, protruding slightly into the entrance, was the side of someone's shoe. Someone was on the other side of the wall. I took a deep breath and composed myself. I was ready. I threw my hand around the doorway and grabbed for the person.

He must have been short because I felt the bottom of my hand brush against his hair before it smashed into the other side of the wall. He let out a yelp and leapt from his hiding place.

It was Tommy.

'Oi, careful mate, you almost took me 'ead off!'

'It's you! That bloody kid from the village.'

'Hey, watch your language I've got sensitive ears.'

'What are you doing here? You scared Baldric.'

'Who's Baldric?'

'He's a horse.'

The kid looked at me blankly.

'Never mind,' I said. 'What are you doing sneaking around here?'

'I need to talk to you. I'm serious about Miss Natalie, she's trouble.'

'She's not.'

The barn door at the other end of the stables opened and Tommy ducked behind the wall.

'You have to listen to me,' said the boy.

A voice came from the other end of the stables. 'Richard, are you in here?' It was Natalie.

'Miss Natalie and Rochdale are in it together,' said the boy.

'In what together?' But he was gone. I heard his footsteps run off into the distance and fade away.

Natalie tapped me on the shoulder. It made me jump, and it wasn't funny, I was crouching and I nearly face-butted the wall.

'Who are you talking to?'

'Baldric,' I said, getting up and brushing bits of hay from my clothes. I smelt like horse and looked like a hobo.

'Have you been drinking that whisky?'

I shrugged, 'I had a sip.'

She slapped me on the arm. Not in an angry way. More of a, "I love you, but you are a nuisance" kind of a way.

'Dinner's in two hours, why don't you go and have a bath and get dressed and I'll meet you in the sitting room for a drink before we eat.'

'Sounds good.'

We walked arm in arm up to the house. It looked like a giant troll crouching on a hill, shielding itself from the sun, the windows glowing like its life gleaming in its eyes.

The sun was dimming.

Chapter Five

I had a bath and put on a dinner suit Natalie had surprised me with.

When I got to the sitting room Natalie was already there. Her hair looked remarkable. She must have been to a salon and spent a lot of money. It was the kind of hairdo that required an architect and planning permission. The kind of hair-do that is so beyond male comprehension that we have evolved in the last few decades to be completely oblivious when a woman gets any kind of haircut, no matter how subtle or grand, just to save our brains from malfunctioning. This is why when a woman says to you, "Notice anything different about me?" while pointing at her extraordinary and clearly different hair do, the average man will say, "New shoes?"

She had two drinks in her hand. Rochdale was with her. He took one of the drinks from Natalie and came over with a big greeting smile and handed me the glass.

'No hard feelings about this morning eh?' I shook my head. 'Good man.'

Natalie was standing at the other end of the room smiling, as if to say, "You see, he's not so bad".

I wasn't so easily fooled. But I accepted the drink. Who wouldn't? This was whisky after all and I'd heard about his expensive taste.

We were standing next to a giant fireplace with an old clock on the centre of a wide mantelpiece. Above it two swords crossed a family crest on a shield. There was a thin brass bucket beside the fire with an array of fire-tending tools in it; a brush on a metal pole, a metal poker, a metal hook, an axe, and mysteriously; a rifle, barrel end down. I bet this house is littered with weapons.

He raised his drink to me and I instinctively clinked glasses with him. He put his arm around my shoulder and we walked over to Natalie.

'I'm sure he's a fine gentleman kiddo,' he said to her. Though he was squeezing my shoulder with a force that seemed to contradict his sentiment.

She smiled at me, 'He's my little gent.'

Little?

The door opened and a finely dressed man entered with grey hair and a face for butlery.

'Dinner is ready,' he said.

A large table was waiting for us in the next room littered with silverware, napkins, flowers, wine glasses, candles, and plates covered with silver domes. It was like we were in some kind of elaborate Disney interpretation of a stately home.

Rochdale sat at the head of the table while the butler, who wouldn't reveal his name to me, directed me to my chair and sat me at the other end. Natalie sat at the chair directly to Rochdale's left. They seemed to extend away from me and I had the feeling of being sat on a slightly smaller chair than he.

Three maids entered the room and, at the butler's nod, simultaneously removed the domes covering our food. Steam arose from our plates like smoke signals. If there were any Native Americans around they could have communicated with our food.

There was no form of grace or indication of when

to start eating, Rochdale just launched his fork into a potato and shoved it in his gob. If it was burning him he was hiding it well. He spoke and steam fled from his mouth. "Always blow your food," that's what my mum would have told him.

'So, Richard, tell me about yourself, what do you do?' A piece of potato fell out of his mouth and landed on his lap.

Natalie answered for me, 'He's a writer.'

I wouldn't have said that. I've never been published. Technically I'm just an unemployed guy with a hobby.

I looked at my plate and moved some peas around with my fork. My wine glass was full. The butler must have filled it without me noticing. He was good. I had a sip, I don't normally drink the stuff but it was nice, easy to drink.

'Anything I would know?' he asked.

'About what?' I said.

'Books I might have read.'

'Moby Dick?' I offered.

'Yes, I think I've heard of that one.'

I realised I had misunderstood the question. Natalie frowned at me and I shrugged.

'How's the food?' he said.

I poked it again. 'It's good.'

I picked up the salt shaker and gave my food a light covering. I ate a sprout. It did taste good. For a sprout. I pointed at my plate with my knife and looked up at the butler. He was standing by the wall like a suit of armour. I appraised him. 'Good food.'

He managed to turn his nose up at me without moving a muscle. I sagged. I don't like all this fuss. I'd rather have a microwave lasagne on the couch.

'Natalie said we have to bond,' said Rochdale.

'Dad!' she said, nudging him.

He rolled his eyes. 'I think it would be good if we got to know each other. If you're going to marry my daughter we should get along. Bond a bit.'

Good god, watching him being nice was like watching a toaster try, with all its might, to freeze bread.

I looked over at Natalie. I could see I had no choice. 'Sounds good.'

'How do you like hunting?'

I dropped my knife and it clattered against my plate. 'No!'

He chuckled. 'Fair enough, it's not for everybody. Why don't you come along to the golf course with me in the morning? We'll shoot a few friendly holes.'

An image flashed through my mind of my bruised and beaten body lying face down by the eighth hole with a golf club shoved up my arse and Rochdale's jiggling body laughing over me.

'Sounds like fun.' I said.

I picked up a potato with my fork and shoved the whole thing in my mouth. Like father-in-law like son-in-law. I figured I'd try and find a connection. Maybe I'll drown him in a toilet.

Natalie clapped her hands quietly with delight. She smiled and started eating.

Rochdale narrowed his eyes at me and picked up a Yorkshire pudding with his fork. It was about the size of a small plate. He opened his mouth as wide as he could and fit the whole thing in there without touching the sides. He closed his mouth and swallowed it without chewing. He grinned.

I gulped. I didn't know exactly what was being proven here but the term "Alpha Male" came to mind. I was game.

I maintained eye contact and picked up a Yorkshire pudding with my fork. I opened my mouth as wide as it would go. I reckon I probably looked like a psychotic kitten with a toothpick stuck in its mouth. I raised the gravy soaked Yorkshire pudding and paused for a moment. His grin widened. Natalie was being distracted by a devious pea and hadn't noticed our silent man-battle. I strained to open my mouth further and went for it.

It turns out my face is also about the size of a small dinner plate. I realised straight away that I had lost. He exploded with a guttural roaring belly laugh. Natalie must have looked up and seen what I was up to, I can't be entirely sure as my face was completely covered by the Yorkshire pudding. I put my fork down and pushed and folded it into my mouth.

'Richard! What are you doing?'

I tried to answer but couldn't so I just shrugged and started chewing. I had a circle of gravy outlining my face and dripping from my chin.

Rochdale was still winding down his laughter when I swallowed. Natalie was staring at me with her arms folded.

'Could I have a napkin?' I said.

The butler began to move but Natalie huffed and stood up. 'I'll get it,' she said to the butler.

'Very well,' he said, and then looked at me just so he could look away again disdainfully.

I smiled at Rochdale. He nodded approvingly.

'Perry', said Rochdale to the butler - so that's his

name, Perry, I'll remember that - 'Go and fetch the special bottle of whisky I keep in my study, the Bowmore 1955.'

Perry nodded and left with the mysterious swiftness of a sudden draught.

I'm no whisky expert but I have heard of Bowmore 1955. My dad always wanted a bottle. Comes in a hand cut decanter in a wooden box (also hand crafted). It looks like a small dark-wood wardrobe. It spends 40 years maturing in a dark vault in the depths of a Scottish distillery and costs about six grand a bottle.

Natalie came back in and gave me the napkin. 'What were you thinking?' she whispered.

I shrugged and wiped my face.

'Why don't we take this into the other room,' said Rochdale, standing up.

I smiled at Natalie. Apparently I have a forgivable face, I've been told that all my life. Once Rochdale had left the room she placed her hand on my cheek and gave me a kiss me on the lips. 'What am I going to do with you?'

I smiled and pinched her bum. She squealed silently and playfully slapped my hand away. We went into the other room.

Perry placed the small wardrobe on the mantelpiece and opened the little doors.

'What's that?' said Natalie.

The butler stood aside and Rochdale took the bottle out with both hands, holding it like something precious.

'Whisky,' said Rochdale, 'very fine whisky.' He opened the bottle and took a long sniff. 'Devine.'

He held the bottle out for me to smell. It smelt like an antique shop after a serious fire.

'Mmm,' I said.

The butler brought over three glasses and Rochdale poured. He handed me and Natalie a glass each and picked up his own.

'To the happy couple,' he said.

We clinked glasses and drank. It was the perfect whisky. Rochdale and I reacted identically, our knees went, our heads went back, we let the warm drink strangle our stomachs, and then blew out the boozy vapour. My head was instantly in heaven. I'm sure Rochdale's was too. Natalie had a coughing fit and nearly threw up and put her barely touched drink back on the table.

'I think I'll stick with the wine,' she said, still coughing.

'More for us, eh, kid?' he said.

He put his arm around me and we clinked glasses again. He picked up the bottle and topped me up.

That's it. I forgive him. I think I love him. I love his whisky that's for sure.

The fire was burning well and we sat at large leather chairs in front of it. There was a small round table next to each chair for our drinks.

Perry came in and offered us some bar snacks; peanuts, Bombay mix, pork scratchings, frazzles. I liked Rochdale's style. When Perry came in with the large tray covered by a metal dome I was expecting something fancy that I wouldn't like, caviar or something, but no, keeping it real; crisps and peanuts.

As we sat there, on the large leather chairs in front

of the fire, I wondered how Rochdale had won me over so easily. I shifted my gaze to him. He was sitting, belly protruding, whisky in hand, broad smile, gazing into the fire. I couldn't imagine him sneaking out in the dead of night to brutally assault a fully grown horse. It puzzled me, but I shrugged it off. Whisky enables you to do that. It removes all worries.

The evening passed slowly. We didn't speak much. We just enjoyed each other's company in front of the fire, getting warm and getting sozzled. After a while Rochdale fell asleep in his chair and Natalie and I quietly made our way up to bed.

Chapter Six

The morning happened in an instant. Showered, dressed, breakfast with Natalie (egg, two bacon, fried tomato, black pudding, hash brown, beans, mushrooms, fried bread; two cups of coffee, one orange juice). I brushed my teeth; looked at my hair in the mirror and questioned my sanity (I have never mastered the subtle art of hair care). On with the shoes. Peck on the cheek (from Natalie) and a wave goodbye as I walked down the porch steps to the main drive. Got into the passenger seat of an old black Rolls Royce and Rochdale started the engine. He gunned the accelerator and pebbles smattered the house as we wheel-span out of the drive. Natalie ran inside and slammed the front door amidst a shower of deadly shingle.

I yawned and had a stretch. I don't like busy mornings, they remind me of being late for school and my dad rushing me to get ready.

'Hold on to your trousers,' said Rochdale.

Rochdale put his foot down and we launched out of the drive onto a country road at an alarming speed. I figured I'd play it cool.

When I was sixteen my older brother had a Citroen Saxo which he had spent thousands of pounds on making it look like a giant melted Airfix model. It went like the clappers. He had replaced the back seats with giant speakers and installed a roll cage and racing bucket seats. He was a dangerous person, my brother, and I feared for my life just being near him. I was prepared for Rochdale. I rested my head and closed my eyes and pretended to snooze.

'Playing it cool, very brave,' he said. I ignored him and carried on pretending to sleep. 'You know what,' he said with a yawn, 'I think I'll join you.'

He wasn't going to fool me that easily. I kept my cool and started snoring. I felt the car begin to coast. He started to snore. He was trying to beat me at my own game. Branches started to smack against the side of the car. I opened my right eye and shot a look at him. Head back, mouth open, drool forming a puddle on his chest, foot down, snoring loudly. A car blasted its horn as it swerved to avoid us. I grabbed the wheel and straightened us up.

'Wake up you stupid son of a bitch!' I shouted.

He laughed but kept his eyes closed. 'I didn't know you had met my mother,' he said.

He pretended to snore again. I checked the speedometer; 109 miles an hour. I wacked him on the chest.

'We're going to die!'

He smiled but still kept his eyes closed. A blind corner loomed up ahead of us. The car was rattling fiercely and I could barely hear myself screaming.

'Stop messing around! There's a blind corner!'

He grabbed the steering wheel with both hands and held it tight. I tugged at it but it wouldn't budge. He was too strong. We were going to crash. At this speed I gave us about three seconds before impact. Last resort, I pulled on the handbrake. The back end spun out and I imagined for one glorious moment us drifting all the way round the corner and sliding to a stop between two parked cars. It was not to be. The wheels screeched and set off a pong of burnt rubber. Rochdale was still pretending to sleep. The great British countryside span past us. The force of the skid pushed me up against the passenger door. We were skidding sideways at the wall. Impact was unavoidable. I curled up into a ball and waited for the crunch.

We exploded through the leaf-covered wall sending bricks, dirt, and mortar flying across a neat lawn on the other side. There was a dull thud and I looked out through my fingers in time to see a rabbit fly off into the distance. We drifted for a bit and then came to a stop.

I uncurled myself and checked my limbs; two arms, two legs, two shoes, ten fingers, head. I was fine. Rochdale snorted awake and stretched dramatically.

'Are we there yet?' he said.

I looked out of the window. There was a path of debris between us and the hole in the wall.

'I don't know,' I said.

I saw a golf buggy drive up a slight incline about a hundred yards away and circle toward us. I watched silently as it trundled closer.

'Ah, good, our escort is here,' said Rochdale

'What?'

The buggy stopped about two metres from the driver side door. A smartly dressed man got out and came up to the car. He opened the driver side door.

'Mr Rochdale, your clubs are ready for you and drinks and light snacks have been laid out in the club house as requested.'

'Good man,' said Rochdale, getting out of the car. He turned to me as he got up. 'Coming?'

I nodded dumbly and got out of the car.

Rochdale and the smartly dressed man got in the

front of the golf buggy and I was made to sit on a pull down chair at the back facing the wrong way. As we approached the golf club two more golf buggies drove past us up to the Rolls Royce. There were two men in each buggy carrying tools; shovels, a mortar board, trowel, rake, garden shears etc. On the back of both buggies were several rolls of fresh turf. They were prepared for this.

I decided not to give Rochdale the satisfaction of seeming surprised. I acted normal. It was a non-event. I wouldn't even mention it. I needed to get the upper hand in our man war. He was already well on his way to establishing himself as the alpha male. I would have to win at golf.

I've only ever played crazy golf. Unless you count the one time I played a golf computer game on my sisters Nintendo Wii. I was doing well on the Wii until I accidently took her two-year-old son out with an impressive back swing. Clocked him right on the forehead. He suffered no major injury but he did start speaking French for a while. He shook it off after a few hours and went back to the Goo Goos and Ga Gas that kids normally speak. (Having said that, the Goo Goos and Ga Gas could have been a manifestation of brain damage? I seem to remember he also started crawling backwards. But lots of kids do that don't they?). Needless to say, I haven't offered to babysit since. I also haven't played golf since.

Rochdale left me at the buffet table while he went off to get the clubs. I ate a prawn vol-au-vent and a tiny cheese and pickle sandwich. Rochdale came back with a small brown battered golf bag with two beaten up golf clubs in it. I think one was a putter and the other a driver. He dropped it in front of me and it fell on its side. A mouse ran out of it and scurried out of the open French doors.

'Your golf clubs,' he said, with a smile.

'And where are yours?'

A young man, dressed like a buffoon, as most golf enthusiasts are, appeared behind Rochdale wheeling a large golf bag with an assortment of golf clubs so vast and unnecessary it could keep a metal smelting foundry in business for a century.

'With my caddy,' he said.

'Right, this is going to be fair.'

'I'll go easy on you.'

The first hole looked like an easy shot. You had to whack the ball about two hundred yards in a straight line and get the ball in the hole. Easy.

There were no clouds in the sky and the sun seemed happy enough to shine all day. The caddy pushed a plastic tee into the ground and placed a freshly polished ball on top of it. He handed Rochdale a hand-held device with a screen on it and Rochdale held it out in front of him. He pressed a button and the device beeped twice. A reading appeared on the screen.

'Mm hmm,' said Rochdale, acknowledging the figure.

He gave the device back to the caddy and held out his hand. The caddy stroked his chin and selected an expensive looking club. He handed it to Rochdale. Rochdale looked at a number on the "whacking end" (to use the technical term) of the club and smiled.

'Very good,' he said.

Rochdale lined up beside the ball and readied his

aim. He wiggled his bum and slightly bended his knees. He swung backwards and I hopped out of the way. The force he came down with made my ears pop. He wacked the ball like he was aiming for a distant planet. The ball shot far and high to the left. It was way out.

'Hah,' I said, 'Rubbish!'

Rochdale chuckled. 'Patience,' he said.

The ball was halfway to the flag, but it was way out to the left, it was never going to make it. But then, like magic, it curved sharply downward and to the right and zoomed down at an almost direct course to the flag, it hit the ground and bounced three times before slowly rolling into the hole.

'Hole in one!' he yelled.

'What?! That's impossible! How did you do that? You cheated. What was that thing you used before you hit the ball? Some kind of GPS thingy?'

'Just a wind gauge. I've played this course a thousand times.'

'Bollocks.'

I sensed foul play but deep down I knew it was an honest shot. Admittedly it was hard being annoyed. It was pretty impressive.

I waited for the caddy to set up my ball but he all he did was remove Rochdale's tee and walk off. Rochdale watched me and waited for me to take my go.

'Well?' he said.

'I don't have a ball.'

'Ah, yes. Hold on.'

He rummaged through his pocket and took out a bright yellow golf ball with a smiley face on it. He threw it at me and I tried to catch it with one hand but it bounced off my wrist.

I didn't have a tee and Rochdale didn't offer me one. I put the ball on the floor and took my stance beside it.

I swung back and wacked the ball as hard as I could. The ball flew straight up and landed with a single bounce three yards in front of me. Rochdale guffawed.

I don't think I'm going to out-man him on the golf course. My plan to win was far-fetched and ludicrous. I switched my putter for the driver (rookie mistake) and reset myself next to the ball. I swung again and wacked the ball far and wide. I took note of what Rochdale had done and tried to repeat it. The ball flew left, hit the wind and curved down and landed about ten metres from the hole.

'Not so bad,' I said.

'It's not in yet, kid.'

I slung my golf bag over my shoulder and marched down the neat green to my ball. I chose the putter and steadied myself beside the ball. I closed one eye for accuracy, realised that impaired my depth perception and opened it again, and imagined a straight line from my ball to the hole. I pulled back and knocked it, not too hard, but firm. It rolled, slowly but surely, straight for the goal. I got ready to whoop but the whooping would have to wait. The ball stopped about half a centimetre from the edge. A slight breeze could have potted it.

'Pah,' I said.

I walked over and knocked it in the hole. First hole and I was already losing by three points.

The caddy rolled down the green in a golf buggy with Rochdale in the passenger seat.

'Hop in,' said Rochdale. 'Hole two is just over the bridge.'

I took my seat on the fold down chair on the back of the buggy. There was a stream separating the first hole from the rest of the course. We bounced and clattered over a small wooden bridge to the other side and stopped at the second hole.

The caddy pushed the tee into the ground and polished the ball on his shirt before placing it. Rochdale selected a club and squared up to the ball.

I had lost interest in the game already and remained seated on the demeaning, back-facing, seat.

As I stared numbly at the ground, waiting for Mr Fantastic to shame me with his balls, (I do mean golf balls of course), a bush, slightly to my right, rustled and said, 'Psst'.

I looked up at the bush and frowned at it.

'Psst,' it said again.

I looked over to see if Rochdale and the pretentious golf-dwarf had noticed. Rochdale and the caddy were squabbling over two identical looking clubs.

I looked back at the bush. I could make out two eyes staring back at me. It startled me at first but I got up and wandered over in a meandering kind of a way to not draw suspicion.

I stopped just beside the bush and looked down nonchalantly. 'Who's in there?' I asked.

'It's me, Tommy,' said the scruffy street urchin.

'Tommy! What are you doing in a bush?'

'Being inconspicuous,' he said.

'What does that mean?'

'I don't know, I'm just a child.'

I thought about kicking the bush but opted for

glaring at it instead. I think he was dumbing himself down just to buffer my pride. I think I'm ok with that.

'What do you want?'

'I eard you was comin ere from listenin through the window yesterday.'

'You were spying on me?'

'For your own good. This should elp you. I made it specially last night.'

A golf ball rolled out from under the bush. I picked it up and examined it.

'It's a golf ball.'

'Yes, just hit it as far as you can, I'll do the rest.'

'I don't understand.'

'My instructions are not hard to follow. Just hit it.'

THWACK! Rochdale hit his ball. I turned and watched it disappear into the sky. It was impossible to track with the human eye. I didn't see where it landed but Rochdale was pleased with the result.

'Ha Ha! Beat that Richie boy!'

Richie. The nickname is back.

'Go on,' said Tommy.

I wandered over and placed the ball on the turf.

'Ok,' I said, 'here goes.'

I wiggled my bum and bent my knees (it worked for Rochdale; it can work for me). I steadied myself and swung a wide arch. I hit it fairly pathetically but it got up in the air. It hung at its peak for a faint moment. I heard something click in the bush behind me. I glanced over. A long metal aerial was sticking out of the bush. I could make out a controller (like one from a remote control car) in Tommy's hand. He flicked a switch.

'What in God's name is happening?' said Rochdale.

I looked up at my ball. It was still hanging at the top

of the long arch it was making towards the hole. A little flap sprang open on the top of the ball and a tiny propeller folded out and started spinning. Over the slow breeze of the wind you could just about hear what sounded like a tiny engine coughing into life. Another flap opened on the back of the ball and a tiny exhaust pipe poked out. It sputtered out a puff of black smoke and bobbed and centred itself. Tommy pushed a lever on the control and the ball shot forward. It didn't travel in a straight line but bobbed and weaved at a ridiculous speed. It got lower to the ground as it approached the hole and dodged to avoid a tree. It buzzed across the fine grass spilling tiny shafts of black fumes on to the neat turf. It stopped about a metre above the hole. Tommy shut the engine down and the exhaust disappeared back into the ball. It hung above the hole for the briefest of moments and the propeller petered out and folded back into the ball. The flap closed and the ball fell neatly into the hole. I celebrated.

'Hole in one! Eat that Rochdale!' I shouted.

Rochdale was looking at me with his arms folded. 'What was that?'

'What?'

'Do you think I'm blind, Richard?'

I knew the nickname wouldn't stick.

'No.'

I stopped dancing.

'Golf balls don't sprout wings and chase holes.'

'Wings? Are you ok Rochdale?'

'I'm fine!'

'Maybe the sun's got to you.'

'Or maybe you're a cheat!' Rochdale loomed over me and snorted like a cartoon bull.

'How could I have cheated?'

I was cowering in his shadow. He narrowed his eyes and backed off.

'CADDY! Next hole!'

'You still have to putt your ball,' I said.

He huffed and grabbed a club at random from his golf bag. He lurched into the driver seat of the golf cart and sped down the green to his ball. He held his golf club out high above him, ready to strike. Rochdale had inadvertently invented a new sporting hybrid; golf-polo. He bounded, wheels kicking up dirt and grass, down the green to the ball and whacked it with all his might. The ball shot out of the golf course and smashed the large stained-glass window of the church. Rochdale dived out of the golf buggy and let it roll into a sand bunker where it exploded into a ball of fire (it didn't really explode but it would have been cool if it did). Rochdale scrambled to his feet, let out a primal scream, and started attacking a tree with his golf club.

The caddy and I shared a worried look.

'Is he always like this?' I asked.

'He has good days and bad days,' said the caddy.

Rochdale threw his bent golf club at a group of golfers on a nearby hole and marched back up the green to us. The caddy and I stood still with fear.

'Ok,' he said, fighting for breath, 'next hole.'

He turned from us and stormed away.

'Good luck,' said the caddy, and ran to catch up with Rochdale.

I looked at the bush to see if Tommy was still there but he was gone.

The third hole passed in silence. Rochdale won by five strokes. I was determined to lose now. If I won, even by accident, I was sure he would kill me. The next few holes passed in a similar manner.

Tommy reappeared at the ninth and final hole. Rochdale had hit his ball into a curve on the course and was taking his second shot down the final stretch up to the flag. I was at the top of the course waiting for my shot when I caught sight of Tommy up a tree to Rochdale's left.

Rochdale had just wiggled his bum, impact was imminent. I squinted at Tommy. He was lying on a branch pointing something long and narrow at Rochdale. My immediate thought went to "rifle" but then my rational mind convinced me otherwise. My rational mind was wrong.

Rochdale swung his club back and came down with a precise swing. Tommy fired the gun and the ball exploded into a cloud of powder. Rochdale dived for the ground. The reverberating echo of the shot rang out across the course.

I glimpsed something swing from a tree to my left and vanish out of sight and Tommy was gone, like a strange and pointless ninja child.

Rochdale was back on his feet and chasing the caddy around the eighth hole waving his club above his head like a confused and deranged Viking.

I laughed. I could think of nothing better to do. I had lost at golf. Rochdale was insane. I was surely going to pay for it and I could think of nothing better to do than laugh. So I did. I really went for it. Rolling on the floor holding my sides, sputtering laughs and asthmatic giggles; hysterical by definition.

I collapsed on to my back and tried to compose

myself. Slow breaths. I calmed down and lay looking at the sky until two shadows landed on me. Rochdale's face eclipsed the sun. He was smiling. I looked at the owner of the other shadow. It was the caddy. He had a bloody nose and a bent golf club wrapped around his head.

'Game set and match,' said Rochdale.

'What does that mean?'

'It means I won! Ha! Undefeated!'

'Congratulations,' I said.

'Club house rules, the winner pays for the drinks.'

He held his hand out and helped me to my feet.

'Cool,' I said.

He put his strong, bear-like, arm around my shoulders and we walked up to the golf club together. Lunacy; it's wonderful.

Chapter Seven

We finally staggered home at 3am. We burst through the tall front doors and sang our way into the entrance hall. Our drunken duet filled the house. We stumbled into the sitting room and Rochdale poured two glasses of whisky.

'Did you see how hard I hit that ball?!' he slurred, 'It exploded!'

'Boom!' I shouted.

He tried to sit on a chair that wasn't there and fell on the floor. We both burst out laughing. I grabbed his hand and dragged him to his feet.

'You're alright, kid,' he said.

I slumped on one of the big chairs by the fire and held my whisky on the arm rest.

Rochdale stumbled toward the little wooden wardrobe, containing the expensive scotch, with his arm outstretched eagerly. He missed by a foot and bumped into the fireplace. He bounced off, avoided a footstool with his drunken ballet, found himself near the door, said the word 'banfamore!' and abruptly left the room. ("Banfamore" is a word used by very serious, and very seriously drunk, drunks, it's the biological equivalent of those small red cards you get from the postman when they can't fit your parcel in the letter box. It means, "I'm sorry but the brain had some trouble getting messages to your limbs, will try again tomorrow.")

I felt like I'd been left hanging. There's nothing worse than being left alone after a good drink with the buzz of the evening still rampant. I could have continued drinking myself into oblivion but he left without a word, not so much as a goodbye.

I sat there, eager for our bonding to continue (and we had bonded somewhat since our initial discrepancies) but bonding was no longer on the menu. I can only assume he was too rat-arsed to continue and left to find his bed. Not an uncommon stance to take at this time of night. Alcohol does, after all, have the habit of relieving one of his usual social etiquette.

So one sat there alone for thirty minutes before one realised one was not to be re-joined by the infamous Rochdale. Look, I used the word "one" instead of "I", see, I can be posh. Maybe I am cut out for this life after all! Or maybe I'm just absurdly drunk.

It was late enough for the house to be quiet with sleep but not so early for it to be pregnant with alarm clocks. I went for a wander of the home. The house was, as they say, dead.

At the back of the house was Rochdale's study. It was filled with great books and paintings of wise-looking men in uniforms with dogs and horses. Three of the four walls were covered with shelves of hardback books with no dust covers.

I have a few hardcover books at home and I always think about removing the dust covers and displaying them proudly on my bookshelf, (my bookshelf being the floor beside the downstairs toilet), but I always feel like such a twonk. If my family came around and saw those books – *For Crying Out Loud* by *Jeremy Clarkson*, *The QI Book of General Ignorance*, *The Shining* by *Stephen King*, *The Goosebumps Omnibus*, *Tripping the Night Fantastic*, (or any other of my greats) – stacked with their covers removed (so they looked highbrow when they are not) they would think I was a pretentious twat. For some reason uncovered books seem more mysterious and studious compared to the same books with the glossy coats still on. I've often thought libraries are magical. All those words like... a bunch of words... in books, all displayed like books on a bookshelf. And it is as lame as that; a shelf of books. But it is magical. All those worlds and lives, even if they are fictional, huddled together like a paddock of galaxies.

I took one down at random. It was *On the Origin of Breweries* by *Charlie Darwin*, or something like that. My brain was dancing behind my eyes trying to avoid any sensible kind of reality. Whatever the book was called I dropped it on sight of something else; another bar. My alcoholic cravings were about to get the better of me. It was one of those discreet bars shaped like a globe of the earth that cost about a hundred quid from Argos but about two grand from your respectable local furniture dealer. I propped the lid open and the contents shone out like that famous golden light from the briefcase in Pulp Fiction.

I dived in, metaphorically of course, I'm not mental, and poured myself a glass of Jura; a light but accommodating whisky from the island of Jura (the same island where Bill Drummond and Jimmy Cauty from KLF famously burned a million quid).

I swished it around the glass as I wandered around the room admiring the titles of hitherto unheard of books. Tiring of words I took rest in Rochdale's posh swivel chair behind his very wooden and well-polished desk. To my booze altered vision, my dual layered 3D effect world view, the desk seemed to be made entirely of floating draws. I banged my head on the desk in an attempt to coerce my eyes into a cooperative alliance and two Identical images fled from each other and bounded back only to pass through themselves and circle my peripheral vision until finally being drawn to a central point. The desks wobbled and blurred into focus and became one.

I put my glass down, successfully, and opened a draw at random but was startled by a tap at the window. My arms flailed. Whisky was spilt. Swear words were uttered.

I pulled off my jumper and mopped at the spreading liquid while simultaneously searching the window for the source of the audible intrusion.

The window slid open with a wooden dragging noise that bore no sympathy for the sleeping.

'Shh!' I said, to whomever was concerned.

A nimble body slid through the gap and presented itself beside me. ''avin a rummage?' said a cockney street urchin.

'Tommy! For Christ's sake!' I said, almost taking him out with my empty whisky glass.

'Weren't gonna hit me with that were ya? I'm here to help, and besides, tis wrong to hit a child so I've been told.'

'What's wrong with you? You do know what year it is don't you? You don't have to sneak up on me with your Dickensian accent, like an evil Oliver Twist, don't you have a phone? Or an Ipad or something?'

'Do you?'

I thought about it. 'No.'

'Wouldn't do me much good then would it? But I

do as it appens.' Tommy pulled out a smart phone from his pocket. On the screen was a map of the area. 'See that blinkin' dot in the middle there?' I did, and said so. 'That's you that is, GPS it's called, tracking you I am. For safety. Need to know where you are. So this is a real book?'

He had grabbed a book from the shelf.

'You've never read a book?'

'Hundreds,' he said, putting it back and choosing another one. 'Cumbersome aren't they.'

'In a booky kind of way, I suppose. How have you read a book having not seen one before?'

'Smart phone,' he said waving his phone at me absently. 'You should get one it would save me a lot of trouble in trying to contact you.'

'I like being off the grid,' I said.

I actually dropped my phone in the toilet last Thursday trying to take a picture of a turd that looked a bit like Terry Wogan. But I'm not telling him that.

'Thousands of books on 'ere. All free they are. Of course, only if they're out of copyright. Read all the classics I ave; Dickens, F. Scott Fitzgerald, Hemmingway, Bronte, Defoe, Wilde. What kind of stuff d'you read?'

'Oh, you know... Bob... Bobkin, Dave Do-Be... Do..., something...' I trailed off and pretended I had found something in a draw. By chance I had.

I found a letter opener that had been crafted to resemble a tiny sword. Hanging off the sharp end was a looped piece of string that vanished into the draw. I un-hooked the string from the sword and tugged it. I felt it snag so I tried a more gentle approach. I pulled it lightly and felt that something was on the other end dangling over the back of the draw. I drew it out carefully, it snagged occasionally but eventually found its way over the back of the draw and out into the open.

'Look,' I said, holding it out in front of me.

I showed it to where I thought Tommy was but the room appeared to be empty of any annoying flat-cap wearing children. I was holding a small yellowy envelope sealed with a stamp of black wax.

Tommy suddenly appeared between me and the desk and grabbed the small letter from my hand. I nearly shit myself at the speed of the determined sneaky little bastard but was impressed enough by his agility to suppress any sudden bowel movements. He was gone in an instant and a table light clicked on in the far corner of the room illuminating the envelope and Tommy's dirty inquisitive face.

I came up behind him and looked down at the envelope in his hands.

'Rochdale's ring.'

'What is?'

'The impression on the wax. His wife gave the ring to him before she died.'

'Oh, how did she die?'

'She was an alcoholic.'

'And it killed her?'

Tommy looked away from the envelope and up at me.

'No, she went to a hypnotist and he managed to stop her from drinking.'

'So what happened?'

'She died of thirst.'

'Oh.'

Tommy opened the envelope and emptied the

contents on to his hand.

'Whoa, you can't do that!'

'Why not? Nobody knows I was ere.'

'Fair point. What is it?'

He turned around and held it up. It was a small piece of card with an old key taped to it. I took the key from him and turned it over. The other side of the card was blank. I flipped it back over and examined the key more closely.

'What do you think it's fo-,' my sentence was cut short by the sound of footsteps coming down the corridor.

'Find out what the key is for!' said Tommy.

He threw the key at me, which I promptly dropped, ran to the other side of the room and slid out of the window, closing it silently behind him as he did with the precision and elegance of a ballerina-ninja.

I slipped behind the door just as it opened. Rochdale's dominating shadow grew up the far wall and stared down at me. I stood there frozen, sure the shadow could sense me with its demonic menace. Rochdale stepped forward and his shadow crept across the ceiling and leered over me. I bent my knees and edged down the wall to get away from it. Rochdale grunted and slammed the door. The shadow vanished. I heard the rustle of keys and the lock turn and click shut. I was trapped.

I climbed out of the window. Problem solved.

Chapter Eight

I woke up just as the sun began its climb over the edge of the earth with bits of hay in my hair and Baldric the horse spooning me. I had a yawn and a stretch and put my pants back on. I ruffled Baldric's mane, made my excuses, and left. Nothing more will be said of our evening together.

I walked around the house to the raised patio area and sat on the wall next to one of the lion statues. I watched the sun rise. It was bright. My hangover was bounding about my skull like an over stimulated baby elephant. I needed coffee and a paracetamol. Maybe even a bath. A slush puppy bath! That would be nice. And breakfast. A full English. With croissants. And a curry.

Time was washing over me and soon the house began to wake up. I dropped off the wall and walked up the steps to the French doors. I saw something move through the gap in the curtains. I knocked. The curtains billowed and the butler was suddenly in front of me. He raised a dour eyebrow at me. The lock clicked and the door opened.

'Perry,' I said.

'Brunch will be served in thirty minutes. A bath awaits you and fresh clothes have been laid out in your room.'

'Thanks.'

The curtains bellowed again and he was gone. I turned to close the door but it had already been shut and locked.

Natalie was waiting for me in the room with her arms folded.

'Hello,' I said.

'And where did you sleep last night?'

'I got locked out and had to sleep in the stables.'

She cocked her head. She didn't believe me. A woman's face can convey more than a man's and her face was saying, quite clearly, "I know you're lying to me, you slept with another girl didn't you? It was that skank barmaid from the pub wasn't it? Well I hope you enjoyed yourself!" Then she noticed the hay in my hair and relaxed. I grinned and shrugged.

'You should have tried to get my attention, or rang the bell. Perry would have answered the door. I don't think he sleeps.'

'I was drunk.'

She gave me a peck on the cheek and told me to have a bath. I did and felt enormously better for it.

Very dapper clothes awaited me on the bed. I put them on. In the full length mirror in front of me was a very well dressed stranger. I looked like the kind of guy Tommy would pickpocket. Smart brown suit; stripes, waistcoat, ruffles, watch on a chain. I turned to get a sideways look at myself. The jacket had tails and my bum looked remarkable. I warmed to the look and couldn't help but grin.

Natalie came in wearing an elegant dinner dress. She looked stunning.

'Richard! Look at you, you sexy man.'

'Thanks, you're looking pretty sexy yourself.'

She threw me on the bed and ravished me. That done she straightened her dress and I straightened my ruffles.

Please take a moment to admire the above sentence. Those nine words equate, I hope (I haven't checked all of literature for a shorter one), to one of the shortest sex scenes in literary history. (Please email me if you do find a shorter one.)

'Why are we getting all dressed up for breakfast?' I said.

'We're skipping breakfast and having brunch with some of Daddy's associates.'

'What? I don't want to do that. Can't we ditch that idea and just, I don't know, do nothing?'

'No. It's very important. And if you really want to marry me you'll have to get on with these people.'

'In what way are they associated with Rochdale?'

'I don't know. They have some kind of elite private club, or something, I don't really know what it is.'

'Rituals and stuff I reckon. Killing virgins, wearing robes, mocking kittens.'

'Powerful, wealthy men, do not mock kittens.'

'And killing virgins?'

'Or that.'

The sitting room had turned into a blur of waistcoats, tweed, and moustaches. The rumble and clatter of conversation and entrées stirred around the room. A silver serving tray with four glasses of champagne on it stopped in front of us and Natalie and I took one each. The tray vanished away.

'I think you're the only woman here,' I said.

'I probably am, and daddy's friends are very protective over me.'

'Great.'

I thought I spotted Tommy's dirty face peering in through one of the windows but it disappeared before I could be sure. That boy is making me paranoid.

Rochdale greeted us like a giant violently happy ape. His friendly slap on the back almost dislodged me from my feet.

'Glad you both made it!' he said.

'Glad to be here,' I said, wiping the champagne I had just spilt from my shirt.

'Daddy, have you told your friends about Richard and me?'

'No, not just yet, best keep that one quiet just for now, eh?'

'You're all going to have to accept I'm a grown woman at some point. I can't stay single forever.'

'I know that, but, well, you know how they are.'

'How are they?' I said.

'Don't you worry about that, lad. You just meet everyone and try and not seem too annoying. I've told everyone you're a writer doing a story about the Rochdale family history.'

This took me aback. I built a frown made of question marks and showed it to Natalie. Natalie pouted.

'Why won't you let me introduce him as my fiancé? I'm sure they'll be happy for me.'

'Let them get to know him on a more mutual basis for now so when we reveal he's your fiancé, at some point in the future, the distant future, it won't be such a blow.'

'Maybe I should just go to the pub and wait for them to go?'

'No! A guest in my house is a guest to the club. I,

or they, wouldn't have it any other way.'

'Who's this then Rochdale?'

A man's hand had grabbed mine and shook it.

'Richard,' I said.

'Richard, you the writer Rochdale was telling us about?'

I nodded.

'Yes, this is him, writing about the family history aren't you, lad,' said Rochdale.

'Yes. Writing about the Rochdale family history,' I said.

'Nice to meet you! I'm Uncle Harry!'

'Natalie's showing him around the estate and whatnot for the weekend.'

He let go of my hand having spotted Natalie behind me.

'Natalie, my girl, how's me old kick in the shorts keeping these days?'

Uncle Harry was like a broader version of Rochdale with a more solid, squarer, jaw and sterner eyes. Like an aging Nordic god.

'I'm fine, thank you Uncle Harry, how are you?'

'Oh, you know me, fit as an Olympic swimmer with a boob job, as they say.'

'Glad to hear it.'

He put his hand on my shoulder and leaned in conspiratorially. 'A word to the wise, you see old Lord Witherbrick over there.'

Uncle Harry nodded over to a man standing by the fireplace staring suspiciously at a painting on the wall. He was frail and old with a beard that looked like it was once a KFC Colonel's type beard, but through neglect the moustache had grown so out of control the ends could have been tucked behind his ears and the tip of his beard dangled between his ankles. He was trembling, either out of rage or fear, it was hard to say.

'He very recently lost his marbles,' Uncle Harry continued, 'so be careful what you say around him. His butler woke him up with tea a few days ago and old Witherbrick attacked him with a lamp. Said he thought he was a lizard in his butler's skin.'

'I'll keep my distance,' I said.

There was a loud scream and I saw Lord Witherbrick jump up onto the mantelpiece and pull the painting down from the wall and throw it at one of the waiters. A few people tried to talk him down but he kicked out and shouted obscenities at them. Finally someone grabbed him by the leg and pulled him down. He was carried out by three men. A moment later I saw him through the window being bundled into a car and driven away.

'You see; mad as a lost compass,' said Uncle Harry, 'No longer seems to trust the help.'

'Yes, well. Let's get the water flowing shall we?' said Rochdale.

'Water?'

'Yes, water,' said Uncle Harry. 'The brown stuff.'

'Ewe,' I said.

'Whisky,' Natalie whispered into my ear.

'Oh,' I said, 'I like whisky.'

Rochdale nodded to a waiter who had been standing patiently beside a rack of bells. The waiter nodded back and selected the second to last bell and gave it an almost inaudible ring. A moment later everyone had gathered and sat at large leather chairs around a polished antique coffee table. I say coffee table, if you got the oldest biggest tree on earth cut it down and took a six inch slice out of it, found a way to polish it to a smooth dark wood finish, and then mounted it on a rather large carved lion's foot (carved from the same tree. In fact on closer inspection it appeared to be a one-piece. Remarkable), and then pissed on the rest of the trees, set fire to a rainforest and celebrated by eating a bunch of rare animals, you would be closer to the description of this table than, "coffee table".

Perry arrived from nowhere and placed seven whisky glasses on the table in front of us and then presented a bottle of whisky that appeared to be wrapped in thin grey papier-mâché. Rochdale raised an eyebrow at it and smiled.

'Very good,' he said.

Perry handed the bottle to Rochdale. I felt a breeze on my neck and the butler was gone. Rochdale placed the bottle in the middle of the table and the elderly entourage began to mumble curiously.

'What's the deal?' I whispered to Natalie.

'Not sure.'

'Rochdale,' said a looming tall gentleman, leaning forward and picking up the bottle. 'This isn't what I think it is?' He removed a monocle from his waistcoat pocket and held it to his eye. 'This surely isn't the real thing?' he asked.

'Who's that?' I said to Natalie.

'David Jones.'

'Really?'

'Yes, why?'

'Name doesn't fit the man,' I said.

He had a pointed face and a clipped voice. His hair was grey around the sides and bald on the top. He wore a very decent brown waistcoat and jacket. He put his monocle back and looked at the cork.

'No, it isn't the real thing, however I would like you all to try it,' said Rochdale.

'May I?' said Jones.

Rochdale nodded. 'You've probably all recognised the bottle by now.'

'It is a replica of the recently discovered bottles of whisky from Sir Ernest Shackleton's hut. Left behind from Shackleton's 1907 Nimrod expedition to cross the Antarctic via the South Pole. Three crates of the whisky were discovered in 2006,' answered Jones.

'Correct,' said Rochdale.

'So what's the big deal?' said a short stump of a man with dark combed back long hair. He was dressed rather scruffily, compared to the rest of the cast, but his hunched nonchalant posture only spoke of wealth. His eyebrows dominated his expressions as he spoke. William was his name. 'This must be the cheapest drink in the house, Rochdale, what's the meaning of this?'

Rochdale huffed and took the bottle from Jones's hand. He filled the glasses around the table and carelessly put the bottle down. 'I want you all to taste it, and *remember* the taste.'

Jones raised an eyebrow at Rochdale and William sagged in his chair and picked up his glass. He downed it in one and plonked his glass back down. 'Now explain,' he said.

'Oh stop being a snob,' said Rochdale. 'How do we all like it?'

Everyone nodded in their partiality.

'It's good,' said Uncle Harry. 'But the price is

hardly a knockout. What did this cost? £100?'

'Less,' said Rochdale. 'But that's not the point.'

'So what is?' said Jones, taking a whiff from his glass.

'As you have all just heard from Jones, three crates of the whisky were discovered buried in ice at Sir Earnest Shackleton's hut. By extracting samples from the original bottles Whyte and Mackay have been able to recreate it exactly and are now selling the resulting drink by the truck load, and that is what we have before us. But, more importantly, those three bottles of the original whisky are still in Scotland and will remain in Scotland for the next week. Those precious bottles are so valuable that no one has even attempted to value them.'

An encouraging nod circulated around the table.

'Are you suggesting-' began William.

'It doesn't need to be said. But yes. I assume I can count on you all as usual?'

The last man on the table smiled. Charleston was his name and he looked like an old British explorer. I'm sure his suit was made of khaki. Or maybe it was a white suit that had yellowed a bit with years. He had thick blonde hair and by far the most exquisite moustache around the table. 'It's about time old man. I've been hoping we'd be on to one of your schemes again soon.'

'There is obviously a time limit on this as the bottles are being shipped back to the Antarctic via New Zealand in the not too distant future. But I think we can work with that, don't you?' Rochdale smiled, and the rest chuckled as if to say, "easy peasy," though I'm sure they weren't thinking exactly that. They were probably thinking, "Two weeks, pah, with my intellect and wit I'll have it by the afternoon". Rochdale carried on, 'Anyway, enough of this for now. We have guests. We will discuss this more openly at an appropriate time.'

Everyone picked up their glasses and chin-chinned.

Chapter Nine

By now I was slumped in my chair having been half drowned by the golden spirit. I raised my glass in front of me and watched it sway back and forth, the liquid climbing up one side of the glass and then the other. I smiled and felt the craving for a cigarette, even though I no longer smoke.

My head lolled - half purposefully and half not - and I smiled at Natalie. She frowned at me. I looked at all the fine gentleman around the table. From my left was Natalie, then Rochdale, Uncle Harry, and then Jones, and then Charleston, followed by a spare chair (I assume to be reserved for Lord Witherbrick), and finally, beside that obsolete chair and directly to my right, was William.

Bravery became me and I stood up, almost knocking the table over, and tapped my glass with my pen, which I luckily always carry with me, along with a notepad, as I am, as has been mentioned, something of an amateur writer.

CLINK CLINK, went the pen on the glass.

Natalie began immediately to tug at my jacket to get me to sit back down and Rochdale bore threatening looks into the side of my head. But I was unperturbed and in love, or just drunk; probably a bit of both. 'I have an announcement,' I announced, 'I know you have all been told that I am a writer making a book about old Rochdale here and his family or some such thing.' I swayed and almost fell backwards over my chair. I regained my balance and carried on. 'Actually, the real reason I am here-'

'Ah! Ha ha, I think you've had quite enough,' said Rochdale. 'Why don't you get yourself off to bed and we can discuss this in the morning.'

'Shh,' I said, lifting my finger to my lips and accidently sticking it up my nose. 'As I was saying. The real reason I am here is because,' Natalie covered her face with her hands. 'Natalie and I are getting married!'

I raised my glass in the air triumphantly expecting everyone to raise their glasses and cheer in delight. Instead, everyone's eyes, except mine and Natalie's, settled on Rochdale.

'You knew about this?' said Jones.

'Excuse me,' said Natalie, standing up and taking me by the hand. 'I'll be back shortly to explain.'

'What?' I said, obediently letting Natalie drag me out of the room.

When she got me out of the house I practically fell down the steps on to the gravel drive. She stood there looking down at me from the doorway.

'What?'

'What were you thinking?'

She had her hands on her hips, as you can imagine.

'Sorry,' I said, attempting a sympathetic smile akin to that of Puss 'n Boots. 'At least it's out there meow. Now, I mean.'

She rolled her eyes. 'Ok. Well, there's not much we can do about it now, but still, you need to get yourself down to the pub and sleep there tonight. Tell Derek to give you a room and say I'll pay in the morning. I'll see what the mood is like here tomorrow and we'll deal with it then.'

She turned around and slammed the door. I blew a kiss at the cold metal doorknocker and stumbled slightly in my attempt to remain still.

'I love you!' I shouted.

I turned clumsily on my heel and walked down the long gravel path out to the street. The events of the evening had sobered me up a bit and my careful stomping enabled me to walk along the gravel drive without toppling over. But I know I was still drunk due to the fact that I had started singing *Oh Danny Boy* at the top of my voice. I don't even know the words to that song. I couldn't even hum the tune to you if I were sober. But I believe the government has installed the song into all of our minds to be unleashed when a particular level of drunkenness is combined with fresh air. For what reason I do not know. I sung, and I skipped.

I quietened down when the pub came into view. I stopped at a bus stop and tidied myself up a bit. I straightened my shirt and pulled up my trousers. I'm not sure at what point they fell down. During the skipping I expect. That could also explain the bruise on my forehead. Yes, now I think about it I do recall falling into a post box at some point.

I rubbed my head with my hand and looked at the pub. I was too drunk to continue drinking, which is a bummer when you're not even at the pub yet. I sighed to myself and stumbled in the twilight to the open door of the pub.

The pub was warm and inviting. I saw Derek behind the bar and waved. He half waved back and then said something to the barmaid. She nodded and took over filling the pint he was in the middle of. The next thing I knew he was helping me over to a bar stool.

'You ok?' he said, 'Did Rochdale do this to you?'

'Do what?'

'I don't know, what's happened to you?'

'I think I'm just drunk.'

Derek got back behind the bar. 'Coffee?'

I nodded. 'Can I sleep here tonight?' I said.

'You'll have to pay for a room.'

'Natalie said she'll pay for it tomorrow. She has to stop Roch and his friends from killing me. I think.'

'What did you do?' said Derek, putting a large cup of instant coffee down in front of me.

'I just told them all that me and Nat are getting married. That's all.'

'The club?'

'Yeah, all the club people! I was like, "me and Natalie are engaged!" And they were like, "whaaat?!"'

'Ok, drink that. Then you can go to bed if you like.'

'Go to bed? No, I think I should drink more. I'm not that drunk. I can still speak pretty well.'

'That's true, but also your trousers are undone and you've already managed to spill coffee down your top.'

I looked down. 'Yes. You speak the truth.' I stood up and tucked my shirt in and did up my trousers. 'Sorry, man, I thought I dealt with this outside. Must have forgot to do up the button, or something.' I smiled and sat back down.

All of a sudden I felt the hairs on the back of my neck prick up. As if someone dangerous was sneaking up behind me. Something flashed in my peripheral vision and the bar stall next to me was suddenly occupied by a flat-cap wearing dirty-faced child.

'Ello, governor! Was hopin you'd end up ere, you don't want to be left with that shifty lot down at Rochdale's! Enjoy the whisky did you? Saw you drinkin it I did, had more than the rest I reckon, still, got you out of there didn't it. Reckon they would have killed you if Natalie didn't help you escape you know.'

'Tommy, please talk slower.'

'Come on, drink your coffee, I want to show you somethin.'

I was going to argue with the annoying ridiculous child but figured it was easier not to. I downed the coffee and the sudden buzz of caffeine almost lifted me, if only momentarily, out of my drunken stupor.

'Alright, what do you want to show me?' I said, getting off my stool.

He led me around the back of the bar, something Derek didn't disapprove of, and down a cluttered set of stairs into the basement cellar. On one side of the cellar were metal barrels, stacked on their sides like wine bottles, and on the other side were metal racks holding surplus boxes of crisps and a few wooden crates of lemons. Down the centre of the room was a gutter (I'm guessing the barrels are prone to spillage) that led to a vacant wall.

'Come on,' said Tommy running to the end of the room and squeezing himself behind the barrels. I was too drunk to question his behaviour, and figured it would be quicker to follow than ask anyway, and squeezed myself after him.

Behind the barrels was mostly just wall.

'This is great,' I said, 'Very cosy. I hope what you're about to show me doesn't involve trousers.'

'What do you mean?' he said.

'I don't know.'

He frowned at me and then turned and bent over.

'I think I'm going to go.'

'Just wait.'

I swayed a bit and then frowned at his bottom. 'I don't understand.'

His knees bent and he seemed to be straining against something. The something gave way with a crack and Tommy stumbled backwards.

'Got it!'

'Got what?' I said.

And then he started to shrink. This, at first, was startling, until I realised he was descending a very narrow staircase which had, evidently, been covered by a slim trap door.

I followed him down and at his request closed the trap door behind me. It was dark for a moment and I could hear Tommy mucking about with something that clattered as he took it off a hook and then creaked like a tiny door being opened.

I had a horrible vision then of us going through smaller and smaller doorways for all eternity. But then the thing in his hand was suddenly illuminated by a match and the small door of the lantern was closed.

He led the way to the bottom of the narrow stairs and placed the lantern down on a stone surface at table height.

We were in what looked like a cave that had been carved out of sandstone. The left wall was made of layered stone and a few of the stones had been removed to reveal pipes and wires. A trestle table had been erected in front of the wall and three small televisions and an old stereo had been placed on top of it with wires running into the holes in the wall.

'Wow, what is all this?'

'Take a seat,' said Tommy, sitting on one of the chairs.

I sat down next to him and he turned all the tellies on and finally switched on the stereo and turned it up.

It gave a hollow kind of hum. Like the sound was originating from a microphone in a cathedral. The televisions were of the type that take a while to come alive. As if they've been rudely awoken from a deep slumber. Like small square plastic old men.

The one directly in front of me, to the left of the other sets, finally formed itself into a picture. It was of Rochdale's empty study. Tommy plugged his smart phone into a USB cable, causing the stereo to go PING, and toggled along a menu. He pressed a button and a picture of Rochdale's study came up on his phone. He thumbed the image to the left and it was replaced by a video feed of another room in the house. The television in front of me changed at the same time. I looked away from Tommy's phone to the television. He thumbed that image away and another one took its place. This time we were looking down on the sitting room.

Rochdale, Natalie, Uncle Harry, Jones, Charleston, and William were all standing now and talking heatedly at each other.

Tommy turned up the volume on the stereo, using his phone as a remote, and their voices went from silent, to a quiet murmur, to a loud and crisp dialogue.

'How do you have all of this?' I said.

'Oh, it's very simple this, boss. Hacked into Rochdale's security network didn't I. it runs through the whole town. I can see into nearly any building I like from ere.'

'Wow,' I said, leaning back in my chair. I frowned. 'Surely the old TV's aren't compatible with your phone?'

'Modifications.'

That was enough to justify all things impossible to me and I began to focus on the screen in front of me. The other two screens displayed the kitchen, where the chef was idly throwing knives at a pig carcass, and the main entrance hall, where Perry was having a staring contest with the wall opposite him and probably winning. I know it's because I was still half drunk but it looked like the wall was shrinking away in retreat.

Tommy and I focused on the screen in front of me.

'Surely you understand our misgivings,' the tall man named Jones was saying.

'Of course! And haven't I done all I can to prevent it in the past?' said Rochdale.

Natalie was leaning against the fireplace with her arms folded. The short bushy eyebrowed man, William, (who reminded me, now I think about it, of Andy Hamilton) chirped in. 'And what do we do if he finds out what we get up to? Eh? What if he calls the police? Or bribes us? I mean, can we even start planning this, this whisky job, with him around?'

Natalie unfolded her arms and stepped away from the fireplace.

'He's a good man, and I don't mean he's a do-gooder. If, and this is unlikely, if he does find out it will probably be a shock, but he won't call the police. At best he'll break up with me and go home.'

'Maybe it's best if you broke up with him now and save yourself and all of us any pain for the future' said Uncle Harry, 'If Richard needs to be silenced you know what lengths we're willing to go to.'

'That's enough!' said Rochdale.

They all stood in silence for a moment. Charleston, who was reclined in a chair, lit a pipe and inhaled in contemplation.

'Any input?' said Rochdale.

'What's he like, this Richard? Honest type of fellow, or what? Is he criminally minded at all?'

'No! He's not a criminal,' said Natalie.

'Well, I don't know, I don't *really* consider ourselves to be criminals, just men with a specialised hobby,' said Charleston.

'I agree,' said Jones.

'What exactly are you suggesting?' said Rochdale.

'Look, I think we should put him through his paces,' said Charleston, taking a match to his pipe and relighting it. 'As you all know, old Witherbrick has once again lost his noggin, we need someone to replace him. We can't do the whisky job without a Witherbrick. What are we without the old cat burglar?'

There were murmurs of agreement all around.

'I'm not sure about this,' said Natalie.

'Look, do you want to marry him or not?'

'Yes, of course I do.'

'Well then! He's either with us or against us!' said Rochdale, gesticulating with a freshly lit cigar.

Not wanting to buck the trend, Jones quietly lit a black cigarette.

'PERRY!' Rochdale shouted, causing Natalie to flinch and the burning end of Jones's cigarette to fall to the ground. Unmoved, Jones re-lit it.

Perry appeared beside Rochdale and said, 'Sir?'

'We're running on empty, Perry, keep on top of things.'

'Already noted and arranged sir, will the Dalmore 25 Year Old Single Malt be acceptable?' he said, lifting a fine bottle of whisky from somewhere.

From my point of view it looked as if Perry had the bottle hidden inside his tailcoat. Although I'm not sure, it seemed to come from nowhere.

Tommy looked up at me.

'You alright? It's a lot to take in innit? All this talk of crime and whatnot, and maybe you bein a potential criminal with them.'

'Where was he hiding that bottle?'

'What bottle?'

'Perry. He seems to be everywhere. Like an efficient ghost.'

'I used to think that too. I looked into it actually, turns out he's just a remarkable butler.'

'Oh.'

On the screen everyone had moved out of shot. Tommy toggled along to find an alternative view of the room. He stopped flicking through the cameras and stopped on an image looking down at the men and Natalie sitting around the large coffee table. There must have been a camera in the chandelier above it.

With glasses now refilled they continued their conversation. Rochdale was speaking.

'I think he's got real scoundrel potential that boy. You should have seen him cheat at golf. It was remarkable, obvious, but remarkable. I can't fathom how he did it, it was so obvious but so impossible, I admire that in a man; the ability to cheat and lie so honestly. You know what I mean?'

'Indeed,' said Jones.

Uncle Harry leaned in to Natalie. 'You know, old girl, this decision really lies on your lap. What do you think? Could he be a part of our little club?'

'I won't pretend it hasn't crossed my mind. I mean, I don't want to stop doing this just for a man.' She stopped and thought for a moment. 'Alright, I think I'll have a glass of that after all. Perry, would you mind-'

Before her sentence had finished a hand, protruding from a well pressed sleeve, glided between her and Uncle Harry and placed a glass of whisky down in front of her.

'Thank you Perry.'

She downed the drink and slammed the glass on the table. The whisky caused her face to do an involuntary impression of a demented Persian cat.

She resumed her natural "Natalie" face and continued. 'Ok, actually, I think he'll be a natural.'

'Fine,' said Jones, standing up. 'I'll arrange a few tests and we'll put him through his paces.'

'What kind of tests?' said Nat. 'Why don't I just ask him?'

'I need to be sure he's not just being a scoundrel for love. We need him to be a natural born rogue.'

'Then it's sorted!' said Rochdale, also standing up.

Natalie, Charleston, Uncle Harry and William picked up their glasses and stood. They all held their glasses out in front of them.

'To the future,' said Rochdale. 'To Richard, to

Scoundrels, to our craft, and to whisky!'

'Cheers!' they all shouted in unison.

They clinked their glasses and drank.

Tommy leaned forward and flicked a switch. The televisions turned off with a dull 'clonk' sound, as old TV's used to, and he switched off the stereo and unplugged his phone.

'What a load of balls.'

'Told you they was up to summin didn't I?'

'Yes. Yes you did.'

I stood up and thought for a moment. After a deep breath a solution to this problem began to come together in my mind. I looked down at Tommy, the dirty street urchin, and currently my only friend (unless you count Baldric) and said, 'I need a drink'.

He stood from his chair and reached up to rest a hand on my shoulder reassuringly. 'Got just the thing,' he said.

Chapter Ten

"Just the thing" turned out to be a chocolate milkshake. He is, after all, just a child, though this fact does elude me sometimes.

We were sitting in the small cafe across the road where Natalie and I had sat for a sandwich and coffee yesterday. It was dark and I was drunk.

'Remind me how we got in here,' I said, swaying over my frothy chocolate milkshake. I chased the straw around the glass with my mouth and caught it. I supped.

'Got keys aint I.'

I sucked the straw until my forehead went numb with brain freeze and then opened my mouth and let the straw fall out. I slid the glass forward and rested my head on the table.

'Not gonna sleep there are ya?'

I looked up at him. 'Where do *you* normally sleep?'

'Secret place it is. Not for sharin.'

'I'm supposed to be sleeping in the pub. I think I'll wander back to the house though.'

'Can't say I recommend that guv.' Tommy was eating his milkshake with a spoon.

'Richard,' said Richard. 'My name is Richard.'

'Richard, don't go back to the house.'

'What do you think I should do about this test thing Rochdale wants to put me through? You know, to be a thief with them?'

'That's up to your conscience init, not much harm in nickin a bottle of booze I shouldn't think. Not for love anyway.'

'I thought you were against me and Natalie.'

'I only said they was up to something, we know what that is now and can start to look at this sensibly.'

'Sensibly? What's sensible about it?'

Tommy carried on spooning milkshake into his mouth and ignored my question.

'You should sleep in the pub.'

'It's closed now.'

'I got a key.'

I picked up my glass and peered into it with one eye. I tried to pour the remaining froth into my mouth but the froth leapt out in its own demented direction and splashed over my face. I put the glass down and looked at Tommy.

'Think you got somethin on your face,' he observed.

I let the milkshake drip down my cheeks. Tommy handed me a napkin and I cleaned myself.

'Do you have a key for everything?'

'Not sure, I think so. I copied Rochdale's master key. Worked everywhere so far.'

'Then why did you break in to the manor through the window the other day?'

'Quicker. And nobody gets by Perry if you go in through the front.'

'Let's go there now and piss on Rochdale.'

'No.'

I got up and wandered over to the counter. I took two quid out of my pocket and dropped it by the till.

'Let's go,' I said.

Tommy grabbed the bottom of my jacket to stop me. I looked down at him.

'I'm taking you over to the pub,' he said.

I was going to argue but a sensible subconscious part of my brain seemed to have adopted Tommy as an authoritative voice of reason. I obeyed pitifully and let him lead me across the road.

Chapter Eleven

I awoke on a hard wooden bench at the back of the pub. My back was aching and it took some considerable effort to raise my head from its hard pillow-less resting place. I groaned and looked around me.

Behind the bar the cleaner, an elderly lady, was helping herself to a glass of scotch from an optic. I frowned. My head ached. The bench I lay on was hidden behind two circular tables so I was able to watch her without being noticed. Having finished the scotch she cleaned the glass and put it away. She then switched on the vacuum cleaner and began to suck the life out of the beer stained carpet.

I rolled off the bench and climbed to my feet using the bench and tables as a kind of drunk man's ladder. She didn't see me stumble toward the back of the pub but must have heard me fall through the fire doors.

Dawn had broken and the sun was low in the sky. I had to shield my eyes from its insolent glare. It took a while to get my senses in order enough to acknowledge that this feeling was just a hangover and not some kind of demon curse.

On the corner of the pavement to my right was a red post box. I noticed a key hole in the little door in the front and fished around in my pocket for Rochdale's key, knowing before I even attempted that it wouldn't work. I absently pushed the key into the hole but it wouldn't fit. It was at least three times too big. I put the key back in my pocket.

The sounds of the morning, up until this point, were

of birds singing their sunny tunes, the electric whir of a milk float slowly making its way down the high street, my own occasional hiccups, and a cat playfully leaping around a small pile of rubbish bags outside the café across the road. The warm early sun and all the sounds combined to create a general sense of pleasantness and serenity. A mouse ran out from under the pile of rubbish and vanished into a neighbouring garden. The cat continued to jump excitedly around the black bags and wagged its tail and meowed in a way that gave me a brief glimpse into its mind; this cat thinks it's the monkey's pyjamas. He believes his awesomeness is total. He thinks he is a big and scary feline. But he is not a big and scary feline, he is a misguided ball of fluff. I watched it through heavy eyelids and a warm forgetfulness came over me. The mouse was leaning against the wall smoking a cigarette, watching the cat with detached curiosity. The mouse noticed me and we both rolled our eyes and shook our heads and then looked back at the dippy cat. But as I said at the beginning of this paragraph, these were the sights and sounds up until this point, at this point there was a new sound.

It entered my senses and shook them out of their comfort in to a hideous expectancy. I didn't look around to the oncoming sound, not wanting to face reality just yet, and just stared over at the cat and waited. The mouse had vanished in my moment of distraction.

It was the sound of a large purring engine. The sound of wide clean tyres supporting the large black bulky body of Rochdale's stretch Rolls Royce. It crawled up beside me and stopped. The rear passenger window slid down and Rochdale's menacing face slowly appeared. It reminded me of my first ever computer as a child. It used to load pictures one row of pixels at a time usually to reveal a demon at the end of a level of Doom or something. Doom! That was a hell of a game. There was a gun in it called the BFG (or Big Fucking Gun). I wish I had one now.

'Hello Richard,' he said.

I groaned and turned to face him.

'Hello Rochdale,' I said.

'Get in.'

The door clicked open and Rochdale shuffled along to make room for me. Defeated by my own weariness I got in and closed the door behind me.

Rochdale didn't speak to me during the ride and neither did Jones who sat opposite us in shadow staring at me like a giant lanky corpse. I narrowed my eyes at him and even scowled at one point. If he thought I was nuts he hid it well. His deep set eyes stood in his skull, unmoving and unblinking, fixed on me. I stopped scowling and tried to ignore him instead. I looked out of the window and watched the grounds go past as we made our way up the drive to the Manor. I could feel his stare the whole time. It made my bones shudder.

When the car stopped Perry opened the door and I stepped out onto the gravel. Natalie was standing in the doorway of the house with a sympathetic smile on her face.

I heard Rochdale get out of the car behind me and I turned to watch Jones unfold himself from its interior. If I wasn't a complete sceptic I would say that Jones was the dead brought back from the grave and injected with stoicism. If you can inject that. Probably not. He's like a well-dressed monument.

Natalie ran down to hug me. I thought about stepping out of the way and letting her fall face forward into the gravel but held her tight instead, surprised that she wasn't furious at me for ruining everything. Then I remembered it was her who was in the wrong and squeezed her as tight as I could. Her tits nearly popped. She squealed and I let her go. Oh yes, my dear, I thought, I know all about your plan to test my thiefyness.

Released from my grip we kissed, but not for long, just long enough to cause Rochdale to storm into the house. Jones curled his lip at me and followed Rochdale inside.

'Hung over?' she asked.

'Actually I feel ok. Do you fancy a drink?'

She narrowed her eyes at me to see if I was serious, I pretended I wasn't and we both laughed.

It's not that I fancy a drink, it's just that I don't want today to happen. I can feel it in my bones that something terrible is on the horizon. No, not the horizon, closer than that, the porch maybe.

I had a bath. Drank three cups of coffee. Brushed my teeth. Got dressed. Checked I was alone in the room and had a little dance in front of the mirror (don't ask me why I did this, the hung-over mind, for me, is a strange one), and finally joined everyone downstairs for breakfast.

Now, the last time I ate at this table you will remember I took my seat on the chair opposite Rochdale at the far end and we had something of a man fight – an alpha male competition if you will - with a spontaneous

Yorkshire pudding eating contest which I lost.

I took the same seat again but this time, instead of feeling looked down on, I felt like I was at a seat to be proud of. I was ahead of the game. It was a game they believed I didn't know I was playing. Natalie took her seat next to Rochdale, Jones was sitting directly to my left, his bony body casting a shadow over his own plate, and there were places made for two other people.

'Before we eat we should wait for the rest,' said Rochdale.

I smiled and nodded. Jones stared forward like a dormant monolith. Natalie shrugged endearingly and flashed a slight smile at me. Rochdale stared into my soul and squeezed his fat fingers around a glass of orange juice.

I felt a light draught touch my ankles and Perry wafted in. Uncle Harry stomped in after him and noisily took his seat next to Rochdale. Tiffany sat delicately next to Natalie and smiled politely at everyone.

Rochdale closed his eyes patiently as Uncle Harry made a calamity of pouring himself a glass of orange juice.

'Have Perry do it you clumsy buffoon,' said Rochdale, under his breath.

'Perry, get out, we don't need help to eat breakfast!' said Uncle Harry.

Perry raised an eyebrow at Rochdale and Rochdale reluctantly nodded. Perry left.

Jones's eyes moved in their sockets at me with the deepest apology conveyed. His eyes moved to Uncle Harry and, with the effect of a king raising his hand for silence, Uncle Harry stopped what he was doing and put the jug down.

'Last night,' said Jones, 'we were all agog with the news of Natalie and Richard's engagement. I think we would all like to apologise for our immediate reaction. We are all very happy for you.'

'Here Here!' said Uncle Harry, raising his juice.

'Quite,' said Jones, turning his great skull at me. 'I would like to offer my personal apology for my own reaction last night. William and Charleston won't be joining us this morning as they have things to attend to but they also offer their congratulations.'

'Yes,' Rochdale butted in. 'We had a long talk with Natalie after you left, and she's managed to convince us.'

'Yes,' said Harry. 'Don't let us old fools get in the way of love.'

'Ok,' I said, and smiled at Natalie.

Of course, I know this is all bollocks. But still, it's better than nothing. Natalie smiled coyly and turned a curl of hair in her fingers.

'Good, now that's behind us we can eat,' said Rochdale.

'Can Sandy come to the wedding?' said Tiffany.

'What?' said Rochdale. Tiffany smiled. 'Sandy's a horse,' said Rochdale, matter-of-factly. And that seemed to settle it.

Two maids entered the room and raised silver domes from the platters in the middle of the table. On three large plates were piles of bacon, sausages, eggs, mushrooms, black pudding, tomatoes, a bowl of beans with a metal handle poking out of it, hash browns, and fried toast. All their lies, trickery and two-facedness, was momentarily forgiven. My hung-over body nearly leapt off its seat to wallow in that fatty delicious heaven.

We ate like starving pigs and with greasy lips and happy bellies spoke loudly about good things. Good food, wealth, love, how we thrashed all those "puny foreigners" - as Uncle Harry put it - in the Olympics; obedient maids, the jealousy of other stately houses over Perry (apparently he's quite a sought-after butler), the new addition to the family – me –, good booze, golf, etc.

And finally we came to something I was expecting and wondering about.

'So, troubling news about the old purse, what, Jonesy old boy?' said Rochdale, in a surprisingly old fashioned tongue.

'Wallet,' corrected Jones, in his stern unmoving manner. 'Yes, and quite a pain.'

Uncle Harry coughed and said, 'Yes, so you lost it, you were saying, yesterday, what was it? At a cafe you said. Completely gone is it?'

'Yes, lost. I think I must have left it at that small cafe by the train station. I phoned them and there's no sign of it.'

I couldn't help but be aware of the forced nature of this discussion. I listened carefully for the inevitable trap I was being led to. The test, I felt, had just begun.

'Oh, sad to hear it. Was there much money in the wallet?' said Rochdale.

'Yes.'

'How much?' said Harry.

'One thousand pounds,' said Jones.

'Dun Dun Dun!' said the voice in my head.

I wanted to gasp, like they used to in crappy

detective shows from the eighties when the wily detective pointed out the murderer, but I managed to contain both my gasp and the rising smirk of disbelief.

'One thousand pounds. Gosh,' said Rochdale. 'And you don't expect to ever see it again?'

'No.'

'And you've stopped looking?' said Harry.

'Yes. The wallet is gone. And that is all.'

Uncle Harry tutted and the breakfast continued. The seed had been planted.

I ran my last sausage around my plate, trying to clean it of all remaining bean juice, and pondered. After the eating of the sausage was complete I'm sad to say I had pondered myself into a limited conclusion. That is, that this is a test, of what aspect of my character I'm not sure, and if I fail the test I will probably be shot. Like Natalie's ex.

Chapter Twelve

Having been formally excused from the table Natalie and I skipped away holding hands like two pubescent penguins newly in love. I was faking it. I mean I love her of course, it's just, well, she's a bloody devious one isn't she? We flitted joyously up the stairs, her ahead of me, and then she stopped and turned to face me.

'Wait!' she shouted, grabbing me by the shoulders (a tad overdramatically I thought). 'Richard, you must go and get the nice glasses from the glass cabinet downstairs, we should celebrate my father and his friend's approval!'

To be honest, that's what I thought we were running upstairs to do. But yes, a celebratory drink was in order and so, with her directions to the room that housed the cabinet with the finest stock, I bounded down the stairs and across the hall while she, my fair blonde haired lady, ran upstairs to await me in our room.

The room across the hall was pretty much a room full of nice things. An impractical room really. I closed the door behind me and walked cautiously around. What a lot of nice shiny stuff. I came to the cabinet described by Natalie, "The gold framed glass one," she had said, "with the nice glasses in it."

This was the one. I turned the small gilt handle and pulled open the door. The door jammed against something on the floor. I looked down.

A wallet.

Well, well, well, what have we here then? I picked

it up and riffled through it. It was just as I expected. There, in the brown folds of leather, was a thick wad of fifty pound notes. I didn't need to count them, there would be twenty of course. One thousand pounds.

A small hand sprung from behind me, took the inside route under my right elbow and snatched the thing from my hands. I span, nearly fell, steadied myself against the trunk of a rather splendid statue of an elephant, reeled from the elephant trunk - thinking maybe Jones had stepped in and the trunk was not a trunk at all but... well, I'll leave that to your imagination, realised it was indeed an elephant, sighed with relief, remembered the sneaky wallet stealing hand, narrowed my eyes, looked to my left, and saw Tommy, the bastard child of the gutter, casually fanning out the one thousand pounds in his grubby little paws like a cunning street-Arab card shark.

'Ah. It's you. Surprise, surprise. What are you doing here?'

Tommy folded the wad of cash and slipped it into his pocket. 'Helpin.'

'I suppose you think I need your help do you?'

'Yes.'

'Can I have that money back?' I said, holding out my hand. 'I'm giving it back to Jones. I'm not playing their games.'

'What money?'

'Oh, for fu-'

'Have to stop you there I'm afraid, young ears and all that.'

'Give me the fucking money.'

'Ah! Now you're definitely not gettin it!'

I tried to give him the stern look of a displeased

father but the look had no effect. Street urchins are unused to such looks. Well, I say it had no effect, it brightened his smile a bit. I sagged and folded to his will. I mean really, without physically rummaging in his pocket – a situation I'm not eager to get into – trying to talk it out of him would be pointless.

'How do we know what they're testing me for?' He raised an eyebrow. 'I mean, if they want to see if I'm trustworthy I should give the money back. But if they're trying to see if I'm an eligible thief I should steal it. Right?'

'Absolutely.'

'So what do I do?'

'Both.'

'Impossible.'

'I'm stealin the money. And the wallet,' he added, slipping the wallet into his back pocket. 'Look at this.'

He removed his iPad from his satchel and switched it on. A live CCTV image of the driveway was being streamed on the screen. He stood next to me and used his finger to flick the video away. It was replaced by a view of the hallway. 'I got me phone plugged into my little surveillance cave back at the pub, and it's sendin the pictures directly to my tablet. Pretty cool huh?'

'Outstanding. Who's that?' I said.

'It's Jones,' he said, and then used his finger and thumb to zoom in on an area behind him. 'And there's Rochdale crouching behind the grandfather clock, see him?'

'Oh yeah. What an idiot, does he really think that clock is big enough to hide behind?'

Tommy zoomed back out and Jones's face was once again dominating the screen.

'They're in the hall waiting for you to go upstairs so they can come in here to see if you took the bait. They're probably expecting you to see Jones on your way past and hand it to him.'

'I can't believe she trapped me. She's the one who nudged me into it, can you believe that?' Tommy shrugged. 'Seems somewhat un-loving.' I said.

'I'll record everything on this, from the CCTV, and show you anything important. Ok?'

'Ok.'

'Oh, and you couldn't do me the smallest of favours could you?' It was my turn to raise an eyebrow. 'You know Tiffany?'

'Yes.'

'I need you to give her something.'

'What?'

He took something out of his satchel and gave it to me. I looked at it and smirked. 'Is this serious?'

'Alright give it back!'

'It's ok, I'll give it to her. You know Tiffany's a moron don't you?'

'Love knows not these things.'

'Oh god, it's scented.'

'Just give it to her.'

'You don't strike me as the type to give someone a heart-shaped card,' I opened it. 'Oh dear, with a heart shaped photo of you pouting in it! I have to say, my opinion of you has just altered quite considerably. Is this your phone number?'

'Yes.'

'I'm going to make a note of it.'

'Look, I know it seems slightly un-manly, but if one isn't willing to seem pathetic for love, then one doesn't deserve to be in love.'

'I'll remember that when I'm trying not to smother Natalie in her sleep. What happened to your cockney accent?'

He ignored me and put the iPad back in his satchel and walked over to the window. 'Don't forget the glasses, guv,' he said, and then slipped out into the world, leaving me, the unwilling criminal, to fend for myself.

'Are you serious about Tiffany?'

He leaned back through the window.

'Not really guv, but you know, if you actually pull this off and marry Natalie then you'll be settin a precedent, you know? Openin the flood gates. Gives me a chance to marry into money too.'

'That's not why I'm marrying her.' He was gone.

I stuffed the card into my back pocket and took the wine glasses out of the cabinet.

Chapter Thirteen

'Jones,' I said, passing him in the hall.

He narrowed his eyes at me and watched me disappear up the stairs. I stopped when I turned into the landing at the top and ducked down to peer through a gap in the stair banister. I saw Rochdale follow Jones into the cabinet room. I smiled at the thought of them discovering I'm a thief after all and then took the heart-shaped card out of my back pocket and slid it under Tiffany's door.

I checked my reflection in a polished vase on the side table and then joined Natalie in the adjoining room.

'Howdy doody,' I said.

'Howdy,' she said back, narrowing her eyes at me 'What have you been up to? You look like you've been up to something.'

'Nothing. I've been up to nothing.'

A sense of glee had found itself in my bones for completely inexplicable reasons. I think Tommy's perfect crime on my behalf has given me a kind of associated adrenaline rush.

'Do you want me to take my clothes off?' I said.

She blushed. 'Maybe a drink first.' I smiled at her and she cracked, went weak at the knees, she grinned with coy embarrassment. 'Stop it,' she said.

'Alright. You pour the drinks.'

I put the glasses down and began to remove my clothes. She tried to ignore me and poured the two glasses without glancing at me. Last thing to remove was my underwear which I took off and flung into a corner. I put my hands on my hips and looked at her. She still managed to keep her eyes from me, which is, frankly, remarkable. Even I struggled to keep my eyes off me. Not because I'm a handsome stud (although that is a part of it) but because naked men don't make sudden casual appearances as often as you might think.

'I'm having a shower,' I said.

'Ok, just go,' she said, waving me away. 'I'm not looking at you.'

'Ok.'

I walked to the bathroom door swaying my hips like Mick Jagger. I could sense that she had turned her head and was watching me, with either lust or bafflement, and I jumped around to face her with hands still on both hips like a superhero emerging from a phone booth having forgot to put on his spandex.

She picked up a pillow and threw it at me. 'Oh, God! Just go!' she laughed.

I trotted into the bathroom and slammed the door behind me.

I had a shower.

Now, that may have all seemed slightly unnecessary, but I had a good reason. I realised that it was important for her to be able to search me for the wallet. So what better way than to give her all my clothes, and a full visible check of my body, and then leave the room to give her enough time to check my clothes fully and see that the wallet is not on my person. Genius, I think you'd agree. Also sometimes one is taken by the desire to be, all of a sudden, starkers. It gives you a feeling of unburdenment (I think that's a new word. All hail the wordsmith!).

Natalie was relaxing on the bed loosely holding a glass of wine. She tilted her head and eyed me curiously.

'What?' I said.

'I'm just surprised you're dressed.'

'I hope you aren't disappointed? Would you like me to get nekkid again?'

She smiled and patted the bed next to her. I obediently climbed on and sat next to her. She rested her head on the headboard and looked at me. Just looked at me, with those big thirsty eyes. If you looked into those eyes long enough you could believe the freshest spring water could pour from them. She turned to pick up my glass of wine from the side table and gave it to me.

'For my future husband.'

I have to say, even though I know she's a conniving liar, the old heartstrings were well and truly pulled. I should say, I had a little think while in the shower, and you know, she is really doing all of this because she loves me, and not because she does not. Still, it is a little demeaning thinking I couldn't cope with the truth and have to be played and tested like this.

We drank and finished our glasses. She took my empty glass and threw it gently to the end of the bed where it landed softly on the thick airy duvet. She had the fairest skin. He lips beckoned me. Plain, perfect, unpainted lips. They touched mine with the softness only a woman's lips can give. Her eyes closed. I know she's sure I close my eyes too when we kiss, but I always allow that second or so before I do just to see the love that those eyes are able to convey even when closed. I closed my eyes and her mouth opened The kiss got serious.

'Natalie!' Our teeth clashed and she pulled away from me. 'Natalie!' came the voice again.

'Who the fuck is that?!' I said, checking my mouth for blood with my finger.

'Daddy, who else? Coming!'

'NATALIE!'

'I SAID I'M COMING!'

'Thank you for the romantic evening.' I said.

She flipped me a playful bird and twirled off the bed. 'Back in a sec.' She closed the door behind her.

'Wanna watch?' came a voice.

I jumped out of my skin. I'm serious, one minute my skin and I were happily looking at the closed door the next minute my skin was hiding in the bathroom and I was in the wardrobe. These sudden frights must stop. Tentatively skin and essence re-joined and I stepped shakily out of the bathroom.

'Give me one good reason why I shouldn't smack you across the back of the head?'

Tommy sat on the bed where Nat had just been canoodling with me and switched on his iPad.

'Cuz, you're kind enough to regret it.'

'I'm going to buy you a bell.'

'I'm sure I'd appreciate it.'

'You could wear it around your neck like a noose.'

'Come and watch.'

I sat beside him and watched.

Chapter Fourteen

Natalie joined Jones and Rochdale in the hall outside the cabinet room.

'What happened?' said Natalie.

'It's gone!' said Rochdale.

'Yes, the bait was taken, did you manage to search him?' said Jones.

'Yes, he didn't have it.'

'You didn't search him properly.'

'He took all his clothes off and had a shower. I searched thoroughly. He did not have it.'

Jones looked at Rochdale and Rochdale shrugged back. Jones turned and entered the Cabinet room. Tommy switched views showing the cabinet room from the inside. Jones entered the room followed by Rochdale and Natalie.

'You see, it's gone,' said Jones.

'Have you checked the CCTV?' said Nat.

'Yes!' said Rochdale furiously. 'The bastard has somehow managed to interfere with it! He walks in, has a look around, and then the image turns to static, next thing you know the image is back, the wallet is gone, and Richard is leaving the room holding only a couple of glasses!'

I looked down at Tommy and he smiled back like an artist proud of his own work.

'What?!' said Natalie.

'I think there is more to Richard than meets the eye,'

said Jones, leaving the room.

Rochdale and Natalie followed him out.

Tommy switched back to the view of the hallway.

'So now what?' said Natalie.

'Well, I guess really we should all be happy about this, he passed the test didn't he?' said Rochdale.

'He proved he is capable of theft, which in itself only proves he is a degenerate, which I never doubted anyway.'

'Charming,' I said.

'Then what was the point in the test?' said Natalie.

'Honestly, it was just a test of curiosity. Is he a thief? If so we would catch him in the act, and he would probably pretend he was on his way to give it back. Is he honest? No. Unfortunately he is much more than a thief. It would appear he is as good at the game as we are. Have you considered, Natalie, that this young chap might be playing some kind of long con on us?'

'Of course not, don't be stupid.'

Jones didn't react to the insult.

'I have to admit,' said Rochdale, 'this is rather unexpected.'

'Well, what do we do?'

'We ignore the wallet. As far as he knows he only stole something that we believed to be missing anyway, it was an easy steal that he knew he could get away with. We need to see how far his talents really stretch under a controlled and open setting.'

'And how are we going to do that?' said Natalie.

Rochdale raised his eyebrows at Jones expectantly, for his own imagination was not capable of arranging such an experiment.

'Leave it all to me,' said Jones. 'Natalie, you go back upstairs and pretend you know nothing, it shouldn't be too hard for you.'

'Don't take your failed experiment out on me.'

'I'm sorry, Natalie, I will keep you updated on the plan. Now, go and act normal.'

Natalie rolled her eyes and headed back upstairs.

'Get out!' I said to Tommy, pushing him off the bed.

'I'm gone! I'm gone!'

And he was. He rolled along the floor, the curtains billowed, and Tommy had vanished. The door opened.

'Everything ok?' I said.

Natalie smiled uncertainly and nodded. 'I could do with a drink,' she said.

Chapter Fifteen

We had a drink in the kitchen – a quick glass of the fizzy stuff – and nattered a bit, during which much skirting around the elephant was done.

'Shame about old Jones's wallet,' I said, testing the subject.

She smiled briefly, 'these things happen.'

We went quiet. For fucking ages.

Luckily Tiffany, all excited about something (I think you can probably guess what it was. It begins with a 'T' and ends with 'ommy'), invited Natalie and me out to watch her mucking about on a horse. Glad of the distraction we obliged.

There is something horse lovers do called dressage. This was my first experience of it and I can tell you it is the most impractical and pointless activity I have ever witnessed.

Tiffany mounted the sandy coloured beast and proceeded to move slowly sideways.

Horses are not designed to walk like crabs. They are designed to walk like horses. At least that is what I thought, but I was proven wrong. This horse was very well adept at walking sideways. It could even prance while standing still. No mean feat.

'I wonder how Baldric is doing,' I said to Natalie, who was standing next to me at the fence.

Natalie was about to answer when an approaching voice from behind answered for her.

'That horse,' said Rochdale, stopping between

Natalie and I. 'Had better hope it's dead.'

I was going to point out the impossible contradiction his statement implied but thought better of it. 'I really like him,' I said.

Natalie happily watched Tiffany do queer things on a horse and ignored Rochdale's barbaric presence. I could see Baldric in his stable staring over at us. His eyes narrowed and I looked up at Rochdale who appeared to be attempting to stare the horse down.

Without moving his horse-killing stare he lectured me a bit on Baldric's inadequacies.

'Frederick the Great of Prussia once said, "I speak French to my ambassadors, English to my accountants, Italian to my mistress, Latin to my God, and German to my horse", to Baldric, Richard, I wouldn't speak Welsh.'

'Right, I see,' I said, though I didn't. 'But why?'

Baldric turned away and disappeared into shadow. Rochdale slapped his belly and yelled, 'Ha! Stupid worthless horse! Why what?'

'Why do you hate the horse?'

'Because he's a scrounger and a bum.'

'He's a horse.'

Rochdale slapped Natalie on the bottom causing her to jump (I found the thought of slapping your own daughter's bottom rather odd, but who am I to judge the elite?), 'I'm going in to town. I'll be back in an hour,' he said.

'Ok,' she replied, without turning her attention away from Tiffany.

Rochdale trod off and I watched him disappear down the drive and start his walk toward town. Having noticed he was gone Tiffany trotted over. 'Where's he gone?'

'Town,' said Natalie. 'Probably to secretly eat ice cream in the cafe.'

'Ok,' said Tiff, getting off the horse, 'I have to meet someone. Will you call me if he gets back before me?'

'Sure,' said Natalie.

'Thank you.'

Tiffany climbed over the fence and ran off down the drive.

'I think I know what she's up to,' I said.

'And what's that?'

I was about to answer when suddenly, like a poltergeist, Perry was beside me (thankfully preventing me from accidentally spilling the beans about befriending Tommy).

'Sir-' he said.

I jumped. 'Holy shit! You scared the crap out of me!'

'I'm sure. Your presence is required in the house.'

'Any reason?'

'Yes,' he replied, and headed back up to the manor.

'Ok,' I glanced at Natalie for guidance and she shrugged. 'I guess I'll see you in a bit.'

'Ok,' she said.

I nodded and followed Perry to the house.

Chapter Sixteen

Jones was waiting for me by the big fireplace. His arms folded and his face like a monk's flip-flop.

'Richard.'

'That's me.'

'Rochdale is out of the house which might give you a chance to gain some brownie points.'

'I'm listening.'

Jones looked me up and down and then settled his eyes on mine. 'There has been something of a mystery surrounding the location of Cyril's wedding ring.'

'Cyril?'

'Rochdale's late wife.'

'Oh. The wife that quit drinking and died of thirst?'

'The very same.'

'Before she died she locked the wedding ring in a safe, the location of which is a mystery, and then hid the key.' I started to rummage through my pockets. 'As she drew her last breath she said these words, "The safe is a portrait of Black Adder's fool." and then she choked on her dry tongue and died.'

'Dying people always speak in riddles don't they? You would think they would be more concise about these things.'

'One would imagine. She was a frustrating woman.'

'Don't let Rochdale hear you say that.'

'He feels the same. What are you doing?'

He was referring to the way I was rummaging deep in my back pocket.

'Hold on, I think-' I felt it touch the tip of my fingers

and grabbed it. I lifted it from my pocket and held it out in front of me. 'Is this the safe key?' I said.

His eyebrows looked down at it and then narrowed at me. 'Where did you get that?' I shrugged. 'You *are* a dark horse aren't you?'

'No, Baldric is a dark horse.'

Baldric. That got the cogs turning. I think I can solve this case even without help from Tommy the devil child.

Jones reached for the key and I pulled it away and tucked it into my top pocket.

'Leave it to me old man.' I turned and put my hand to my chin in a contemplative manner. The walls in the room were covered with paintings. I scanned them all quickly. None contained what I was looking for. 'Next room,' I said. He followed me into the dining room. I glanced at each painting without slowing my pace. The painting I was looking for was not in there. 'Not in here,' I said, and headed straight for the door at the other end. I went straight in and with a quick glance established this room would also not contain the painting. 'This is the kitchen,' I said, and turned back around.

'What are you looking for?' said Jones, stopping me with his large bony hand.

'A painting of Black Adder's fool.'

'It's gibberish. Adders do not hold court. They cannot have fools. The woman was mad. And anyway, we have checked all the paintings. There are no snakes and no jesters. Nevertheless we checked behind each one and found no secret safes.'

That deterred me slightly. His absent knowledge of British comedy aside, if they really had checked behind each painting without luck maybe I was wrong.

'Why is it important to find the ring?'

'Sit down.'

I sat on the corner of the table. He raised the corner of his lip and I got the message and pulled out a chair instead. He stepped forward and folded his arms. I looked up at his shadowed eyes.

'Do you want to marry Natalie?'

'Yes, of course-'

'The only way anyone is marrying that girl is with Cyril's wedding ring. Rochdale promised her that.'

'Then we must find the safe!' A thought struck me. 'Tell me Jones, why does Rochdale keep Baldric the horse when everyone quite clearly hates him?'

'He was Cyril's. She was the only person the horse ever cared for. Why do you ask?'

'Did she have a photo of Baldric per chance? One she kept on her bedside table perhaps?' You'll agree my mind was on top form with that little question. A nifty bit of prophetic deductive questioning. If she did love the horse she probably had a photo of it, if she had a photo of it she probable kept the photo on her bedside cabinet! Oh yes, Sherlock would be proud!

'No, why do you ask?'

'Oh. Not a picture anywhere then?'

'What has the horse got to do with the safe?'

I stood from my chair and began to pace back and forth in front of Jones explaining the connection with Baldric's name and Mr Bean's early incarnation as Black Adder. I was like Poirot in the final chapter of an Agatha Christie novel. The penny dropped and Jones stood. Well, he didn't stand, he was already standing. He just seemed to stand more if you know what I mean?

'We'll check the master bedroom before Rochdale gets back,' he said.

There we were, like mischievous useless criminals, him tall and bony, me average and normal, rummaging through a dead woman's lingerie draw.

I closed the draw I was rummaging through, having not found a picture of the horse, and turned to Jones who was staring into an open draw with a look of disgust on his face.

'What's wrong with you?' I said.

'Knickers,' he replied.

'Here, I'll look through her knickers and you check the wardrobe.' He did as he was told without quarrel. 'Tell me Jones-'

'Richard, stop talking like a fictional bloody detective.'

'Right oh,' I guess I had got a bit carried away with the role. 'If you were Rochdale, and for some reason hated your wife's favourite horse, what would you do with her beloved picture of said horse?'

'Good question. What *would* Rochdale do with the picture- hold on,' He turned to me with a broad smile on his face. 'That mad old bat!'

'I'm not sure I follow.' Jones took two steps toward me and grabbed me by the shoulders. 'The horse!'

'Yes, the horse, you've managed to grasp the backbone of the thing-'

'The pub!'

'I'm game! But you've lost me.'

'Come on.'

Honestly, the way he left the room, it was like

watching one of those rocks at Stonehenge suddenly break formation and dance out of Salisbury plain.

Chapter Seventeen

It was with great effort that I managed to keep up with Jones on the jog down to the pub. His long legs meant that even a fast walk for him is a serious exertion for me. It was for this reason that I was out of breath when we stopped on the corner opposite the pub. And it is why I said the following unintelligible sentence.

'Wait, hugh, I whew jus...'

'What's wrong with you boy?'

I sat on the floor and put my hand on my chest, 'Jus... haagh, hold on a sec.'

Jones picked me up by the armpit and dragged me across the road. 'Enough of this silliness,' he said. 'This is important,' he went on. 'In there, dear boy, is a portrait of that godforsaken horse of yours.'

'He's not my horse.'

'Well nobody else wants to take ownership of the blighter.'

'You don't like him either?'

'Bugger.'

'The horse?'

'Rochdale is in there.'

'Oh I see.' I stood on tippy toes and looked over Jones's shoulder to see in through the window. 'Oh good god,' I said. 'He really is insane isn't he?'

'If you knew that boy he was holding up against the wall by his neck you would understand perfectly.'

'Yes, I imagine that boy has the ability to easily rile a guy.'

'That is an understatement. Come on.'

We entered the pub. Jones first, me second.

'Rochdale, old chap, everything on the level?'

Rochdale dropped Tommy on the floor and Tommy, after he landed, raised an eyebrow to someone in the back of the pub. I followed his gaze and saw Tiffany was sitting on a lone chair in a darkened corner. Ah, well, now this all makes sense.

'Jones! This runt of a boy is trying to dirty my youngest daughter!'

'Tiffany, did he touch you?' said Jones.

'No,' she said, folding her arms. 'Daddy made sure of that.'

I left them to it and started checking out the paintings to find one of Baldric. Of course I ordered a whisky first.

'Derek, how's things?' I said. He shrugged. 'Whisky please.'

I remembered my manners and looked over at Rochdale and Jones to offer them a drink. 'Rochdale,' I shouted, and then stopped for a sec to admire the view. Jones was holding Tommy upside down by the ankles and Rochdale was trying to get close enough to punch him, something made nearly impossible by Tommy's frantic gnashing. If Rochdale did get close enough for a punch he would surely loose a testicle to the biting child. I shouted louder, 'Rochdale!' he looked over. 'Drink?'

He gave me the thumbs up. Jones looked over expectantly and I raised an imaginary glass in the classic pub born mime that means "want one?" He nodded in the affirmative and I ordered two whiskies on the rocks.

The drinks got placed down and I drew a ten pound

note from my back pocket and paid Derek. As he walked down the bar to the till something extraordinary was revealed to me. In the centre of the back wall of the bar, for all to see, was a large portrait of a slightly harassed looking horse. It was my new friend and cohort, Baldric.

'JONES!' I shouted, surprising myself with my own volume.

He dropped Tommy in surprise and almost lost a toe to Tommy's wildly gnashing teeth.

'What?!'

'Blackadder's fool!' I said, pointing at the painting behind the bar.

'Blackadder's fool?' said Rochdale, clearly recognising the term. 'How do you know about that?'

'I'll explain later,' said Jones, winking at Rochdale. Rochdale nodded and tapped his nose conspiratorially. "Ah, a test," said the gesture.

Jones came and stood beside me and looked at the painting. 'That's him alright,' he said, and then lifted the wooden hatch at the end of the bar and went behind it.

Derek didn't seem to mind this intrusion behind the bar. He just leaned against the wine fridge and watched with interest.

Rochdale came and stood behind me.

'Hello,' I said.

'How did you figure this out?' he said, eying me up and down. 'If this is right I will have a whole new respect for you dear boy, I've been looking for that damn safe for years. Of course, you know what this could mean for you?'

'That I can marry Natalie?'

'I've already agreed to that.'

'What then?'

'It means you can't be trusted.' I opened my mouth to say something but couldn't think of anything. He spoke again. 'Now, that's not necessarily a bad thing dear boy. I don't mind a bit of cunning in a man. It's loyalty that really makes a man.'

'I'm too afraid of you to be disloyal.' I said. Although I'm not sure what loyalty to a future father-in-law/psychopath really entails. Helping to steal a rare bottle of whisky one suspects.

Jones removed the painting and there it was. An old safe with a simple keyhole and handle.

'Derek, break it open!' demanded Rochdale.

'Now, hold on Rochdale,' said Jones. 'Richard, if you wouldn't mind.'

Rochdale looked down at me and I smiled nervously back. I reached into my top pocket and recovered the key that I had found in his desk.

'Where did you get that?' I tapped my nose and winked. He grabbed me by the throat and began throttling me. 'Where did you get it you gob-shite!'

'Rochdale, put him down! If we are to progress as we intend with the boy a certain amount of mutual respect is in order. Don't you think?'

Rochdale let go of me and I dropped to the floor. I crawled behind the bar, choking from the strangulation, and stood up next to Jones.

Jones stepped aside and I put the key in the hole. It turned easily with a click. I pulled the handle down and the safe door swung open. We all stared silently at the contents of the safe. Rochdale came behind the bar and stood between me and Jones. He reached forward and picked up the single item that occupied it. He held it in front of him and we all stared at it.

'There it is,' he said. 'You know, I had this cut by the most expensive jeweller in London and proposed to the old girl in a gondola in Venice.'

Rochdale looked up at Jones, for affirmation I think. Jones nodded and Rochdale turned to me.

'If I give you this you must promise me one thing.'

'What's that?'

'You will marry Natalie and never let her down, and anything you discover, or become involved in, with me or any of my associates will remain a secret until you die. And if it does not remain a secret until you die you *will* die. Understand?'

'That's two things.'

'Yes or no?!'

'Yes!'

He handed me the ring. It was incredible. One large diamond in the middle with a pattern of small diamonds around it, creating the effect of a rose, all set in a white-gold ring. It was beautiful. I put it carefully in to my inside Jacket pocket.

'Right then,' said Rochdale. 'We have things to discuss, do we not?'

'Indeed,' said Jones, following Rochdale out from behind the bar and toward the pub doors. 'I'll contact the others.'

'Good. Tiffany! Get back home and do not leave your room. Understand? TOMMY! I'll deal with you later.'

Tiffany nodded and ran out of the pub ahead of us. Tommy said nothing.

Chapter Eighteen

An old posh car was pulling into the drive as we arrived back at the house. Charleston and William got out of it. Rochdale, Jones, and they, shared greetings and we all entered the house together.

Natalie was waiting for us in the tree coffee table room. I took the seat next to her and Rochdale took the seat to her left. Next to Rochdale sat Jones, and then Charleston, and to my right sat William. Two chairs were left vacant.

Natalie put her hand on mine and squeezed. It felt like a worried squeeze so I smiled at her and winked. The idea of this wink was to instil a sense of security, it was meant to say "It's ok, it's all under control". But she looked at me as if the wink had said, "guess what, I'm drunk and stupid." But I wasn't drunk. However, I was hoping the bottle of whisky Perry had just entered with would change that.

Perry placed glasses in front of us, already laden with ice, and filled them.

'Are we going to wait for Harry?' said Charleston.

Rochdale looked around the table and then down at the glass. It seemed etiquette meant not drinking until things were under way. 'We'll start without him,' he said, picking up his glass.

William nodded to Charleston and Charleston removed a large rolled up piece of paper from a tube and unfurled it on the table. Charleston used his glass to weigh his corner down and William used his glass for the far corner and my glass to weigh down the corner nearest me. The nerve! How will I drink it now? William looked at Rochdale, clearly expecting him to use his glass to weigh down the final corner. Rochdale narrowed his eyes at William and slammed his palm down instead. With his hand now safely securing the corner he sipped at his whisky and smiled.

'Ok,' said Charleston. 'As you can see these are the floor plans, or blue prints if you will, for the Whyte and Mackay distillery.'

I was listening, but I was also staring at my drink. I decided to copy Rochdale and so held my corner down with my left hand and took the glass in my right. Rochdale noticed and raised his glass slightly. I raised mine back and had a sip. Charleston continued.

'Now, William and I have been up to the distillery and have taken the tour. We have the whole thing planned out.'

'Before we continue,' started Jones, looking at me. 'Should we not enlighten our newest member as to what it is we do?'

'Ah yes,' said Rochdale, looking at me. Natalie squeezed my hand again. It was at this point, due to the hand squeeze, that I realised I had let go of the blueprint which was now curling back toward the middle of the table. William huffed and flattened it out again. He took a pocket watch from his pocket and used that to thwart the curling.

Rochdale frowned at this and then at his hand which was still holding his corner. He put his whisky down and removed a harmonica from his jacket pocket and used it as a weight. A harmonica? Can you imagine this man slowly whiling the nights away with the blues? Never judge a book by its cover, eh?

'As I was about to say,' said Rochdale. 'Jones, William, Charleston, Uncle Harry and I, and Natalie of course, are all part of a very exclusive and secretive club.'

Jones butted in. 'You won't be aware of this but we have been testing you over the past few days to see if you had the right character to join us.'

Rochdale took over. 'Marriage to Natalie, Richard, comes with automatic membership to this club. So we had to make sure you were right for it. You know?'

Now it was William's turn to add something, 'We're not bad people you understand, and we weren't trying to see if you were bad-'

Rochdale retook the helm, 'We needed to see if you had a scratch of the scoundrel DNA in your blood.'

'You have it in spades,' said Jones.

'We won't embarrass you by revealing what the tests were. You're smart enough to figure that one out for yourself,' said Rochdale.

'There's nothing worse than the feeling of being caught out,' said William.

'Let's just say we were very impressed and haven't the foggiest how you pulled it off,' said Charleston.

Rochdale winked at Jones and Jones smiled back.

'Let's just say you owe me £1000. I can't prove it. But we all know you do!' said Jones. The four of them (Natalie had more compassion) laughed.

'How in God's name did you steal that wallet Richard?' said Rochdale. I shrugged, so much for not revealing anything to save my embarrassment. 'I mean, somehow you got around the CCTV and managed to get the wallet past Jones and me and made it disappear before you got to Natalie's room. Tell us how you did it, lad.'

'And the safe key. We never even expected you to solve that one. It was to test your loyalty to Rochdale. No one snoops on the house of another member-'

'That is a line that one does not cross!' said Rochdale.

'However, you have to be let off the hook for that one. How on earth did you already have the key for the safe?' said Jones.

I opened my mouth to answer but thought mystery would serve me better.

'Fair enough, we all have our secrets. But one day you must enlighten us,' said Rochdale.

'What safe?' said Natalie.

'Richard. I think it's time for you to present something to your future wife. Don't you?'

'Oh, yes, of course.'

I slipped my hand into my top pocket.

'On your knee lad,' said Rochdale.

'He's already proposed,' said Natalie.

'He's doing it again,' said Rochdale.

I got down on one knee. I held her left hand in mine and looked up at her. I decided not to ask her verbally, it didn't feel right, and besides she had already said yes. I raised my right hand and opened it. In my palm was the stunning white-gold ring with the diamond rose. Natalie's hand went to her mouth in surprise. She paused for a second to catch her breath and slowly took the ring from my hand.

'Mummy's ring,' she said, still breathless. 'How did you find this? We've been looking for so long.' She stopped speaking and just stared at it.

'Try it on kid,' said Rochdale.

Natalie gave me the ring and I slid it on to her finger. It fitted perfectly. There was a moment between us then that I can't explain. If I had more time in that moment I might have been able to capture it in words. Sadly, Rochdale was with us.

'Right! Good, sit down Richard,' said Rochdale. I obeyed. 'Now, Natalie, as you know this is to be your wedding ring so you can't keep it on.'

'Ok,' she said.

'Perry will look after it until the wedding. We know it will be safe with him.' There was a slight breeze and Perry was behind Natalie, ready to take the ring.

Natalie took the ring off, looked at it one final time, and then at me. Her eyes shone in that moment, like a perfect cliché. She handed the ring to Perry. Perry nodded, tucked the ring into his top pocket and wafted away.

'Thank you Richard,' she said.

She looked me in the eye, a smile climbing up her cheeks, and then she lurched forward and embraced me tightly. I hugged her back, just as tight, and she sobbed.

'I love you Richard. Thank you,' she said.

'I love you too.'

She let go of me and tried to regain some composure. She tucked a curl of hair behind her ear, wiped a tear away with her sleeve and downed her whisky. That's my girl.

'Ok, back to business,' said Jones, struggling to hold back the sobs.

'You ok Jones old boy?' said Rochdale.

'Of course, I'm fine! Got something in my eye... oh God, ok I'm just a sucker for romance.' He blubbered and Perry appeared beside him with a hanky. Jones blew his nose and wiped his tears away. He downed his whisky and lit one of his black cigarettes. He practically smoked the thing in one puff, which was quite impressive, and put it out on the blue prints.

'Finished?' said Rochdale. Jones nodded and straightened up. 'Ok then, back to business. Charleston, please continue.'

'Ok. If you look here on the blue prints, next to Jones's cigarette burn, you'll see there is a service entrance to the goods-in office-'

Once again Charleston was interrupted. But this time it was a noise coming from the hall. It sounded like someone was banging randomly against the walls while occasionally swearing.

'Harry! Is that you? What in the hell are you doing?'

'Come on you bastard!' came a reply. There was another bang and the sound of something expensive, a vase maybe, smashing on the ground. 'Shit. Sorry Rochdale.'

'What was that?'

The bangs were getting closer now and Perry skimmed over to the door and held it open. He ducked in time to avoid the end of a long aluminium ladder.

'I have a better plan,' shouted Uncle Harry as he clumsily got the ladder into the room. 'Ignore whatever convoluted, impractical, Oceans 11 style, plan these idiots have put together.' He dropped the ladder on the floor and put his hands on his hips triumphantly.

'Well?' said Rochdale.

'A ladder!' said Uncle Harry.

'I can see that,' said Rochdale. 'What's the plan?'

Uncle Harry walked up to the blue prints and put his finger down on a room. 'This is where the bottle is. See this window?' Everyone nodded. 'We put the ladder to the window and get the bottle. Easy.'

'The window is locked from the inside,' said William.

'And how do you know that?' said Uncle Harry.

'We checked it when we were on the tour.'

'Fine then we'll take the tour and unlock the window from the inside. Rochdale can help our new cat burglar with the ladder and voila.'

'Cat burglar?' I said, but was ignored.

'That's pretty much what we had planned,' said Charleston.

'Good! Then we're all in agreement! So when do you want to do this Rochdale?'

Rochdale shrugged, 'Book yourselves on to a tour and we'll do it tomorrow. Perry, you're driving getaway. Have the limo ready.'

'As you wish, sir,' said Perry, with a nod.

Chapter Nineteen

It is not my wish to gross you out, but, well, how can I say this without seeming crude? After the little meeting around the table Natalie dragged me up to the room and gave me the best loving of my life. It was like the genuine physical manifestation of love had erupted out of her and I was the benefactor of its ecstasy inducing gift. I could barely move afterward. I was in a sex coma. Sweaty and dehydrated, I laid on that bed. My body buzzing with endorphins. I could hear Natalie whistling happily to herself in the shower. I tried and failed to wipe the smile off my face. My life could have ended in that bed and my life would have been complete.

If only it had ended there. A tap came at the window and surprise surprise there was Tommy's mucky little face grinning in at me. He gave me the thumbs up and motioned for me to open the window. I pulled the duvet over me and gave him the finger. How much did the little bastard see? He rolled his eyes, wrote the word "Horse" on the window with his finger, and disappeared.

Natalie finished with her shower and I jumped in and had one myself. When I came out Natalie was sleeping with a big smile on her face. I got dressed, chucked the suit I had been wearing back on - it is a wonderful suit - and headed out to the stables.

Tommy was sitting against Baldric's stable door. Baldric was facing the other way staring into the corner like a sulking child.

'What's wrong with Baldric?' I said, as I approached.

Baldric's ears sprang up at the sound of my voice and he turned with a joyful trot and came to the stable door.

'He's such a weird horse. He really likes you,' said Tommy.

I petted Baldric and gave him a Polo mint. 'What do you want Tommy?'

Tommy stood up. 'Think he'll let me pet im?'

'I don't know. Give him a Polo first.'

I handed Tommy a Polo and Baldric tentatively ate it out of Tommy's hand.

'I wanna ride him!'

'I don't know if he can be ridden. Do you know how to ride a horse?'

'Sure. Do you?'

'No. I guess you just sit on it and the horse pretty much does the rest.'

'Pretty much. A good orse is pretty intuitive, so I've eard.'

'But this is Baldric. He's not your average horse. I notice you've reverted back to the Cockney accent.'

'True. Are you suggesting some kinda falsery on my part?'

I gave Baldric another Polo. 'Why did you ask me to come out here?'

'I want to know about Tiffany. Have you seen her? Has she mentioned me?'

'I haven't seen her. She's been locked in her room.'

'I'm in love with her.'

'You're a child. You don't know what love is.'

'You're an adult and you're hanging out with a horse and a child. You've agreed to steal a very rare and expensive bottle of whisky to prove you love a woman you barely know. You can't possibly be in a position to advise me on anything. Especially love. Innit guv'

'Eloquently put. But adding "innit guv" to an otherwise well-spoken sentence does not a Cockney make.'

'Love changes a man my dear boy.'

'Give it a rest you bizarre corrupt infant. And I don't "barely" know her. We've been going out for nearly a year. And also, I have to admit a personal curiosity as to the taste of the original Shackleton Whisky. It's not all to please Rochdale. Although I am a bit nervous about stealing it. I've never nicked anything before.'

'Don't worry guv. I've got a plan that will keep your conscience clear.'

'What is it?'

Tommy tapped his nose with his finger. 'You just carry out the robbery as planned and I'll make sure, if you lot get caught, you will be innocent without question. Got it?'

'I don't trust you.'

'You have no choice, I've got your back whether you want it or not. Now, all I want you to do in return is to quietly unlock Tiffany's door. That's all. Alright?'

'I'll unlock her door but I would feel far more comfortable knowing exactly what it is you intend to do?'

'I intend to romance her.'

'Not with Tiffany. What do you plan to do to ensure my innocence?'

'You just gotta have faith governor! Don't worry about it.'

I decided to leave Tommy at this point. I gave him the remainder of the Polos for Baldric, Ruffled Tommy's hair, and bid him adieu.

'Don't forget to free my maiden!' he shouted after me.

'Yes, yes, I won't forget.' I said. And I didn't. It was the first thing I did. I walked upstairs, quickly and quietly turned the key in her door, and then headed to Natalie's room. I opened the door and peeped in just to check she was still asleep. She was. Good.

Tommy had got me thinking. I realised I didn't have to commit a crime at all. All I had to do was not make the switch. The plan was for me to climb the ladder, switch the old bottle with a new one and no one would be any the wiser. All I have to do to avoid committing a crime is to climb up that ladder, wait for a bit, and then do nothing. I just pretend I switched them. Sorted.

I thought I'd go downstairs and have myself a drink to celebrate.

Chapter Twenty

'Richard! What are you doing down here?'

It was Natalie. Evidently I had fallen asleep on the tree-table and when she shouted, "Richard! What are you doing down here?" I awoke with a start and fell off it. I landed on an empty bottle of whisky which goes a long way as to explaining my chosen bed for the evening and the throbbing feeling between my temples.

'Get up! Breakfast is being served in the dining room and then we have to go. Everyone thought you had done a runner in the night.'

'I was celebrating our love, my dearest,' I said, with a smile that took some effort to create.

She grabbed me by the arm and dragged me to my feet. I suddenly felt great, god knows why, maybe it was the rush of being lifted to my feet so quickly. A kind of bliss came over me. 'What's for breakfast?' I said, 'Bacon and eggs I hope! Or maybe even some melon! That would be nice. And orange juice! And coffee!'

'Come on you idiot. It's a full English.'

I licked my lips. 'Mmm, have you eaten? You look lovely. How do I look?'

'You look like a tramp in a suit.'

I looked down to see that I was still suited and booted from yesterday. Marvellous! Saves the job of getting dressed today!

She got me into the dining room and sat me down at the end of the table where I normally sit, right across from Rochdale at the other end. Everyone was there. Rochdale, Jones, Charleston, William, Uncle Harry, Natalie, Richard (that's me). I smiled at everyone and picked up a sausage. I realised at this point how drunk I still must be. Not a thought of the events that are planned for today have worried me thus far. Good, perhaps I'll have another drink before we head out.

'Good, you found him,' said Rochdale. 'Did you find Tiffany?'

'No,' said Natalie.

'She's probably with Tommy,' I said.

'If she is I'll kill the little bastard,' he said.

'I'm sure she's fine. I've asked Derek at the pub to keep an eye out for her,' said Jones.

'That will have to do for now. We can't reschedule everything just because she's run off again.'

'And besides,' said Charleston, 'the whisky is being shipped back to the Antarctic in a few days.'

'Ah, yes, I had forgotten about that. Shall we get going then?' said Rochdale. 'What is it, a six hour drive from here?'

'About that,' said William.

'Perry!' shouted Rochdale, but before he even finished shouting the word "Perry" Perry was in the room.

'The car is waiting, sirs.'

'Splendid!' said Uncle Harry, getting up first.

Chapter Twenty-one

Everyone slept on the car journey. I was surprised at this at first, but then, considering the average age of the group (which is, by my own estimation, about forty-two thousand), I guess it makes sense that they might take the opportunity for a nap. This gave Natalie and me the chance to talk.

'So you're a professional thief,' I said.

'It's not like that.'

'So how is it? Drink?' I had found a refrigerated compartment in the limo that had a bottle of Champagne in it.

'We can't, that champagne is to celebrate on the way back. It's hard to explain.'

'No that makes sense.'

'Not the champagne, *how it is* is hard to explain.'

'You've lost me.'

'You asked me if I was a professional thief.'

'Oh yes, I forgot. I didn't ask, I observed. Can we drink these?' I had found two cold bottles of beer.

'Sure.'

I opened them using a nifty trick I had learned in my teens, where you pop the cap off with a lighter, and gave one to Natalie.

'So how did this all come about? Surely you're all rich enough to not need to steal?'

Natalie swigged from the bottle. Rochdale had started snoring. Natalie put her hand on mine and smiled at me. 'This is nice isn't it? Me and you in a limo, enjoying a cold beer together-'

'Four aging aristocrats napping, on our way to a robbery, it's very romantic.'

'You know what I mean. It's all out in the open. Daddy and his friends have accepted you, and I think Jones has taken quite a liking to you. You found mummy's ring. And I was worried about how you would take to all this, you know, finding out what the club gets up to, but you seem to be ok with it. It's just this is the first time since we got together that the wedding seems like it could really happen.'

I swigged from my beer. 'What makes you think I'm ok with this? The only reason I haven't run for the hills is because I love you. And because your dad is a psychopath who would probably track me down and kill me with his bare hands if I did run.'

'Probably. But this really is just harmless fun. Daddy and his friends have everything. There is nothing they can't afford to buy. Life is complete. It's boring. So they make it interesting again by obtaining those things that can't be bought. And it is quite exciting isn't it?'

I thought about it and smiled. 'It is exciting. Do you want to have sex?'

'Here? No! What's wrong with you?'

'The daring of what we're doing is making me horny.'

'When we get back I'll give you the best loving you ever had.'

'Deal.'

I looked out of the window. The scenery was passing by without incident. This, I knew, was the calm before the storm. 'How much farther do you think it is?'

Natalie shrugged, 'Not far, twenty minutes maybe.'

'I'm nervous.'

'It will be fine, these old farts are consummate professionals. I had better wake them up.'

'Do you have to?'

Natalie leaned forward and tapped Rochdale on the leg. He grunted. 'Daddy!' she said, tapping him again. He stirred but didn't wake up and did that weird thing with his lips that old sleeping men do, like they might have a mouth full of food and have to start chewing just in case but stop after a few seconds when they establish the mouth is empty. Natalie reached forward and slapped him across the face. His eyes shot open and his hand immediately went to his inside jacket pocket.

'Uh uh,' said Natalie, and I noticed she was delicately holding a revolver.

'What? Why did you wake me up?!'

'We're nearly there.'

'Where?'

'Whyte and Mackay.'

'What? Oh, of course. Give me my gun back.' Natalie handed it back. 'You're lucky I didn't shoot you.'

'It's not luck, daddy, I've been avoiding getting shot by you since I could walk.'

'Well, I'm sorry about that. You know how it is.'

'Yes daddy.'

'Perry, coffee,' said Rochdale. The coffee pot next to the fridge I had found the booze in clicked on and started filling with the hot brown stuff. 'Jones, William, Charleston. WAKE UP!'

'Good god!' I said, 'Loud enough?'

'Ha, you've got weak ears lad.'

'You've got a big gob,' I said back.

'I will shoot you Richard. You know I have a gun. Just because you've had my blessing doesn't mean you're safe. You did see me attempt to shoot my own daughter a moment ago just for waking me up didn't you?' I smiled nervously but didn't say anything. 'Good. Now, as Perry is driving would you mind making us all coffee?'

'Of course,' I said.

I made coffee. Charleston, Jones, and William, yawned, stretched, and rubbed their eyes.

'How far, Perry?' said Rochdale.

'We're just turning in now, sir.'

'Harry! Are you awake?'

The answer came from the passenger seat next to Perry, 'Yes! I'm too buzzed to sleep!'

'Good. Drink up lads, the game is on.'

Chapter Twenty-two

You're probably thinking that a limousine isn't exactly the most inconspicuous vehicle in which to carry out a heist. And you'd be right. However, it is a perfect vehicle to transport a very long ladder. We stopped in a lay-by just before the entrance to the Distillery and Rochdale and I untied the ropes that had been looped around the entire limo in order to fasten the ladder to the roof. With the ladder removed the rest of our consort carried on to the distillery without us. The plan was for our respectable colleagues to turn up in the guise of wealthy whisky connoisseurs (which of course they are), take the tour, which William had already arranged, and unlock the window. The plan, when they get into the room containing the Shackleton Whisky, is for Natalie to pretend to sprain her ankle and then as a double distraction, for William to pretend to choke on a piece of nicotine gum and faint. Once all are distracted Charleston will unlock the window and then I simply pop in, switch the bottles, and nip out again. Easy.

Rochdale and I watched the limo disappear around the corner and up the drive to the distillery.

'Ok, come on lad,' said Rochdale, picking up one end of the ladder.

I picked up the other end and we made our way around to the back of the old distillery.

'What's Uncle Harry's job during all this?'

'He's the muscle.'

'Muscle for what?'

'Put your end down I think this is it.'

We had stopped beside a curved wall. I remembered it from the blueprints. The curve of the wall kept us just out of sight from the yard and the loading bays we knew to be around the corner. At the top of the wall, about three stories up, was a single window.

We propped the ladder against the wall and extended it to its maximum height. It stopped just short of the window.

'You'll be able to get in from there won't you boy?'

'Yeah, no problem.'

'Good. Because we'll need it if we get caught.'

'Need what?'

'Muscle. Uncle Harry. Keep up lad, you asked the question.'

'Oh, do you think we will get caught?'

'Not a chance.'

'Where's Uncle Harry now?'

Rochdale nodded over my shoulder. I turned but didn't see anything.

'What?'

'By the entrance.'

I stepped out to get a look around the side of the building. 'What the fuck?'

'You see, we're covered if anything goes wrong.'

Uncle Harry was crouched behind a decorative bush right by the main entrance. In his hand was a double barrelled shot gun, and (I shit you not) in a sheath on his back, was a sword.

'This is insane.'

'Right, Richard, get up the ladder and peep through the window.'

I climbed up and peeped like he said. 'No one's in

there yet.'

'And the key?'

'In the lock.'

'Good. Now we just wait.' I ducked down and waited for the sounds of distraction. 'Richard, can I ask you a serious question?'

I looked down at him, 'Sure, what is it?'

'This is awkward. Your wedding to my daughter-'

'Yes?'

'Well, do you already have a best man lined up?'

I have to say a brief smile of disbelief crossed my face. 'Rochdale, are you asking me if you can be-'

'Don't be stupid.'

'So what are-'

'Jones asked if I would ask you. He seems to be quite taken by you.'

An involuntary laugh escaped me. 'Jones wants to be my best man?'

'What? It's not so funny. He's never been a best man before.'

'Hold on. This is a lot to take in.'

'Yes or no!'

'Quiet, old man, we'll get caught.'

'Yes or no?'

I relaxed a bit on the ladder. 'Does he really like me?'

'Yes. And god knows why.'

'I'm flattered.'

'Richard, I'm waiting for an answer.'

'Well, I don't have anyone in mind. I mean, I was going to ask my brother but, I'll decide when I'm back on level ground if that's ok?'

'Fine. Any sign of them yet?'

I peeped again but the room was still empty. 'Not yet.'

'There are benefits to having Jones as your best man,' said Rochdale.

'Such as?'

'The stag do will be unbelievable. He may come across as the serious type, but the man knows how to throw a party.'

'That could sway me. Wait, I hear something.'

I peeped back through the window. They were just entering. I ducked down and pointed frantically at the window to convey the news to Rochdale. He nodded and gave me the thumbs up and then put his finger to his lips. I gave him the thumbs up in acknowledgement and then did the zip across the lips motion to express my understanding of his wishes further. He nodded, and we waited.

Chapter Twenty-three

Natalie screamed. It had started. A loud manly choke came after the scream followed by a thud (presumably the sound of William falling over). Then came the sound of rushed footsteps followed by the sound I had been waiting for. The click of a key being turned and a single tap on the window to let me know everything was set. I looked down at Rochdale and gave him the OK signal and he nodded. Now all I had to do was wait for them to leave the room, sneak in, and pretend to switch the bottles. The spare bottle! Shit!

I quietly climbed down the ladder to much confusion on Rochdale's part, and stopped at the bottom.

'What are you doing?' he whispered.

'Where's the spare bottle?'

'Ah, good lad, good memory, Uncle Harry had it, hold on.'

Rochdale snuck off and I watched as Uncle Harry drew his sword, fearing an attack from behind, and nearly took Rochdale's head off. There was some urgent mumbling and then Harry left his hiding place and disappeared, supposedly to the limo. Rochdale turned back to me and shrugged. Moments later Harry was back, looking flustered and annoyed, with the bottle. Harry retook his place and Rochdale hustled back to me.

'Here. Now get up that ladder and do your bidding!'

I climbed back up the ladder and peeped into the window. The room was empty. The window slid open with little effort and I climbed in. It was official; from this moment on I was a criminal.

There it was. The genuine 1907 bottle of Shackleton's whisky. Just lying there in a glass topped refrigerated case. I opened it and took the bottle in my hand. I compared it to the fake in my left and was impressed by the likeness. After comparing the two I un-thievingly put the original straight back in the fridge. Like hell was I going to steal something that valuable!

I put the bottle down on the window shelf as I climbed out onto the ladder and then reached back in to get it, almost knocking it over, and held it above my head in faux triumph. Rochdale punched the sky and beckoned me back down the ladder.

'Show me it lad!'

I gave him the bottle and he studied it carefully. 'You devil! You did it you devil! Come on, we've got to get back to the lay-by.'

We retracted the ladder, took an end each, and made our way back.

Success!

Chapter Twenty-four

We got back to the lay-by and were surprised to be met with stern faces rather than beaming smiling ones.

'Problem?' said Rochdale.

'Yes!' said Uncle Harry. 'This very nearly went very badly thanks to your daughter and her new boyfriend!'

Rochdale looked at me and then at Natalie.

'Not that daughter,' said Jones.

'I'm sorry, I'm not sure I follow,' said Rochdale.

Jones stepped aside and opened the limo door. Revealed inside, staring back at us, were the dirty cheeky face of the boy Tommy, and the deeply concerned face of Tiffany.

'What are you doing here?' said Rochdale and I simultaneously.

Tommy smiled and shrugged. 'Thought we'd tag along for the adventure,' he said.

'When I went back to the limo to get the whisky I found Tiffany trying to half-inch it for herself,' said Uncle Harry. 'And then Tommy came prancing out of the main entrance like a demented bloody gazelle!'

'I was just happy,' said Tommy.

'How did you get here?'

'In the boot of the limo,' said Tiffany, with a sob.

'Don't you give me those crocodile tears young lady, you are in big trouble.'

'I must urge that we leave and deal with this when we arrive back at the manor,' said Jones.

Rochdale thought about this and then nodded. 'Get

out of the car.'

'What?' said Tommy.

'You heard me. Get out!'

Tommy and Tiffany got out. 'How will we get back home?' said Tiffany.

'The same way you got here!'

Rochdale went around and opened the boot of the limo. 'Get in. We'll deal with you when we get back!' Tommy and Tiffany clambered in and Rochdale slammed the boot. 'Scene over, let's go!'

Everyone got back in the limo and we set off back towards Rochdale Manor.

'Are you ok?' said Natalie.

'I'm fine. I'm not really sure what the deal is with Tommy and Tiff. What are they doing here?'

'I don't know. I told you that boy was trouble.'

There was a pop followed by a fizz and I looked away from Natalie's perfect blue eyes to see that Rochdale had cracked open the champers.

'We will not let this little hiccup get in the way of celebrating a smoothly executed heist!'

'Here here!' said Charleston.

We were all crammed in; Jones, Rochdale, Charleston, William, Uncle Harry, Natalie, and me. A part of me thought Perry should get to join in on the celebrations, but I guess someone had to drive. Once we each had a flute of champagne in hand we raised them high and Rochdale said, 'To keeping the soul alert and the liver yellow, cheers!' We all said cheers and drank. By the time we got back to the manor, several hours later, we were all completely sozzled.

After we had parked, and managed with little drama to extricate ourselves from the limo (only two of us fell drunkenly out of the vehicle; me and William, everyone else managed to get out more or less like a sober person would).

Rochdale opened the boot. 'Tiffany, you go to your room.' Tiffany climbed out and ran for the house. 'And you, Tommy boy, are spending the night right where you are.' Tommy raised a finger to protest but Rochdale slammed the boot before he could start.

'Shall we have another drink?' I said, with a slight stumble toward the house.

'Another drink? Dear boy, we have business to attend to!' said Rochdale.

'Business? What business?'

Jones lumbered up next to me and placed a hand on my shoulder (for support I think) and said, 'Important club business.'

William stumbled past me and stopped beside Rochdale, who was himself swaying slightly, and held up the bottle of Shackleton Whisky. Natalie elegantly tripped up beside me and then proceeded to use me as a crutch. Her hair was all a mess, her demeanour was askew, and her actions were drunkenly flirtatious. 'That business,' she said, pointing to the bottle.

'Ah,' I said, and then fell, bringing Jones and Natalie collapsing down on top of me. Seriously, what were they expecting to happen? A drunk can't use another drunk as a prop. It's absurd. It's like using a flamethrower to put out a burning house. Just not as bad. I guess it's more like using a book as a bookend. Or a jellyfish as a hard hat. No, that last one doesn't make sense. Damn these similes, I've lost track of where I am. Where was I? Oh yes, on the floor.

Luckily Uncle Harry was at hand to drag us to our

feet.

Chapter Twenty-five

We convened in the tree-table room. Perry had laid out seven espresso shots to help with our concentration. We drank them - having all taken our seats - and Rochdale ordered another round, which Perry promptly served.

'Alright,' said Rochdale, 'drink these tiny coffees and we'll crack open our trophy. One needs to be at least moderately sober in order to properly enjoy such a rare treat.'

We did as he bid and drank our tiny coffees. I'd never actually had an espresso before, but my god, it was like drinking a full fisted punch between the eyes. I can't say I became entirely sober, but the all-out drunkenness of moments before had become a fond memory.

Rochdale put the stolen bottle of whisky on the table and then Perry appeared with one of the Whyte and McKay copies and placed it next to it. There was a clear difference between them, which was odd, considering I had faked the switch. They were both essentially the same. Both were wrapped in faded paper and aged for faux authenticity. The bottles were the same shape and colour. But the bottle Rochdale had put down genuinely looked old. The paper that covered it was almost transparent and was torn around the neck. The one Perry placed down was clearly new by comparison.

Our espresso cups were collected by Perry and replaced with whisky glasses.

'We'll start with the copy to remind us of its taste. Are we all happy with that?' said Rochdale.

We all agreed and nodded to express said agreement, except me, I just stared at the old bottle, bemused and miffed. The copy bottle was opened by Perry and he filled our glasses. We drank. It tasted exactly as I remembered. It was a light easy whisky with a wisp of smoke that breezed over your tongue after the swallow. A delightful and outstanding whisky.

Rochdale was savouring the taste, still rolling it around his tongue before swallowing. He looked at the empty glass in his hand and nodded. 'Really not bad for a replica,' He said.

Uncle Harry clumsily put his glass back on the table. 'Come on Rochdale, stop delaying, let's get to the good stuff, eh?'

'Agreed, stop teasing us, old man,' said Jones.

William leaned forward, 'May I do the honours?'

Rochdale raised an eyebrow at William. 'No,' he said. 'The honour goes to Richard. You did a fine job out there lad.'

'Here, here!' said everyone, except William, who slumped back dejectedly.

'You don't mind do you?' I said to him.

He shrugged, 'No, I guess you have deserved it. Go on lad, open the bottle.'

Rochdale was holding the bottle out to me. I leaned forward and took it. As I grabbed it Natalie caught my eye. She was smiling like I'd never seen before. It was a proud smile. She put her hand on my knee and squeezed. 'Love you,' she mouthed.

I stood up and Perry breezed over to me holding a

corkscrew. I took it and screwed it in. Wait, a corkscrew? I looked at the other bottle which stood open next to Rochdale. Its screw-top lid lay on the table next to it. I looked back down at the bottle in my hand. I was gripping the bottle in my left and was poised to pull the cork. Holy shit! This was the real fucking thing! What the fuck?

'Everything ok?' asked Rochdale.

I looked at him, my mouth agape. 'Yeah, just a big moment,' I said.

Rochdale smiled. 'It is, and we're all waiting to taste our prize.'

'Ok,' I said. 'Here goes.' I pulled the cork and it came out easily with a satisfying "pop".

'William, do you want to do the pouring? I'm afraid I'm too shaky,' I said.

William lit up. 'Hand it to me, it would be my pleasure.' He poured the glasses and for a moment we all just sat there staring at them.

'Only two living people in the entire world have tasted what we are about to taste. One of them is Whyte and Mackay's master blender, Richard Paterson, and the other is the renowned whisky writer, Dave Broom. We are about to enter into a very exclusive club.' Rochdale picked up his glass.

After a moment, after what was said had sunk in, we all took our glasses. A feeling of nervous anticipation swarmed around the table. Even Natalie, who wasn't a great whisky drinker, was exhibiting a nervous and excited smile. We all raised our glasses, half expecting Rochdale to say something before we drank, but there was nothing to say, there was only to drink. Normally on this occasion there would be at least a vocal

"Cheers" but there wasn't even that. The moment was too special to be tainted by a drunkard's salute. Instead, Rochdale gave the glass a slight raise, like a salute to the god of Whisky, and we all did the same. And then, all at once, we put the glasses to our lips and drank.

If the Nobel Prize had a category for blending whisky then Richard Paterson would be a household name right now. The taste, when compared to the replica, was identical.

Charleston, who had been quiet until now, put his glass down first and put his hand to his chin in contemplation. 'They're the same,' he said.

Rochdale nodded and Jones picked up the 100 year old bottle and had a sniff. He then picked up the replica and had a sniff of that. 'Remarkable. They really are the same.'

'I'm not sure if this is an anti-climax or something to be applauded as a great achievement in the art of whisky blending,' said William.

Rochdale poured himself another glass and raised the bottle in a, "anyone else" gesture. Everyone held their glasses out for more. Perry took the bottle and topped us all up.

'Who cares if it tastes exactly the same,' said Rochdale. 'There are now nine people in the world who have tried it and we make up seven of them.'

'Cheers to that,' said Uncle Harry.

The moment of sublime that prevented us from saying cheers earlier had passed and we all raised our glasses and shouted a loud, 'Cheers!'

Jones lit a thin black cigarette and those that smoked joined him. Rochdale and Harry lit a big cigar each, Charleston lit his pipe, and William rolled a cigarette.

The veil of wonder at this prized possession had quickly turned from a moment to savour to an event to celebrate. Natalie leaned in to me and kissed me on the cheek. I put my glass down and kissed her on the lips. It was a long kiss. For a moment it was just me and Natalie in the room and all that mattered was her lips. This feeling soon crumbled to the sound of applause. I stopped kissing her and we were met with a standing ovation. Rochdale, Jones, Uncle Harry, Charleston, William, and even Perry, were all standing and clapping. The applause settled down and Rochdale raised his glass for a toast. 'To my future, cat burglar, son-in-law!' They all raised their glasses and gave the mandatory "here, here!" and drank.

Even though I was fairly certain I had purposely bungled the theft I had apparently bungled the bungle. Interestingly, and I'm not proud of this, because of the praise that was flooding my way from these drunk aging aristocrats I was full of pride and became secretly glad the theft had gone, somehow, to plan.

The initial singular awe of the Shackleton Whisky had now faded enough for us to be able to drink the remainder of the whisky more liberally. Perry brought another bottle of the replica to the table to keep us going.

It wasn't long before the men were asleep, Natalie was unconscious (she wasn't used to such massive volumes of the golden stuff) and I was implausibly the last man standing. I poured the last drop of the old whisky into my glass and with great effort removed myself from the tree-table room.

Chapter Twenty-six

Rochdale's car was still parked haphazardly in front of the house. I stood swaying in the open doorway and had a sip of my whisky. The key for the car had been hanging on a hook inside by the front door. I stepped down on to the gravel and pointed it at the trunk. I pressed the boot opening button on the key fob and the indicator lights flashed and the boot clicked open. It raised slowly to reveal Tommy, curled up, watching me on a CCTV monitor displayed on his iPad.

'Took your bloody time,' he said, climbing out and stretching his back.

'I'm very drunk, Tommy, so go easy on me. I may well urinate on you if the mood takes me.'

'It's 5am! I've been in there six hours!'

'It's your own fault really.'

Tommy shut the boot and took the key out of my hand. He ran into the house, put the key back on the hook, closed the door and re-joined me outside. 'Come on, we'll go to the stables. Perry never goes out there.' I don't know what Perry has to do with things, but the stables are always a comfortable place to be drunk. 'Perry's still awake, and believe me, you don't want anyone to know it was you who let me out.'

'Right, yes of course. Let's go.'

In the stables Baldric looked splendid. His injuries had all healed; no bandages, no limp, just a big horse, albeit a horse with a slightly weird expression. But that was just Baldric. Maybe that's why no one likes him. It's a look that if you saw it on a human you would think it meant, "I've just done something weird and you don't know what it is. Maybe I had sex with your slippers, maybe I farted in the ice cream. I know, but you never will, bwa ha!'

We went into Baldric's stable and sat together on a pile of hay. Baldric trotted to the other side of the small pen and sat down opposite us. Bum down, hind legs sprawled out in front of him, front legs dangling, and a weird smile on his horsy face.

I went to drink out of my glass but realised I had finished it. Unless I hiked back to the house drinking for now was done. 'Alright, you little freak,' I said to Tommy. 'Why were you at the distillery?'

'First tell my how the tasting went.'

'They tasted the same.'

'And nobody thought that was weird?' he said, with a smarmy look on his face.

'No, they thought it was a remarkable tribute to Richard Paterson's Blending expertise.'

'You're speakin very well for a drunk.'

'I'm well-versed.'

'So they were similar, the two bottles. Would you say they were identical?'

'What are you getting at?'

'You want to know what I was doing at the distillery?' I nodded dubiously. 'Two reasons. One, it was mine and Tiffany's first date. And secondly, I know how you feel about stealing so I made sure you wouldn't have to.'

'Weird place for a date. What do you mean you made sure I wouldn't have to?'

'We had a picnic in the boot, it was actually very

nice. I switched the bottles.' He grinned.

I looked at my empty glass. I had a vague idea
where this was heading and thought a drink would
probably be useful afterward. Either for drinking or
pouring over Tommy and setting fire to.

'Go on,' I said.

'I snuck in to the room that had the old booze in
after Jones and the other two left. I was hiding in the
hallway behind a black and white cardboard cut-out of
some shabby looking bloke with a beard.'

'Sir Ernest Shackleton.'

'I dunno. But anyway, I got in and hid behind the
fridge with the old whisky in. After a few minutes the
window slid open and you climbed in. After you stole
the bottle you put it on the window shelf while you
climbed back out. That's when I made the switch.'

'Oh god.'

'I took the replica that you had replaced the original
with and switched them back! You never actually stole
anything! It took seconds. I grabbed the old bottle off
the window shelf, put the replica in its place and then
put the original right back where it belonged!' I stared
at him. He stared back with a wide proud grin on his
stupid face. I narrowed my eyes. 'Well, what do you
say? You're not a thief after all!'

'Tommy, you little nitwit-'

'Hey, how dare you, after all I did for you –'

'Tommy! I never actually made the switch. I just
pretended to. I went in with the replica and left with
the same replica. The original never moved from the
fridge!'

'What are you saying? We both had the same plan?'

'Yes.'

'Oh.'

'Two people trying to thwart the same theft in the same way can only lead to the theft being carried out exactly as planned. Your kind actions to stop me stealing have caused me to unwittingly steal after all. Thank you.'

'So, I thought I was switching them back, but I was actually making the heist go exactly as planned.'

'Yep.'

'I helped you steal a priceless 100 year old bottle of whisky?'

'Yes, Tommy.'

'How exciting!'

'You're a twat, Tommy. A nuisance, and a twat.'

'You realise a twat is a woman's-'

'Tommy. I know what a twat is.'

'What do we do now?'

'Any ideas Baldric?'

Baldric's ears pinged forward, his tongue fell out, and his tail began to wag.

'Do you think Baldric thinks he's a dog?' I said.

'Almost certainly,' said Tommy.

Baldric's ears changed direction and his eyes narrowed.

'I think he heard something. What is it boy?'

Baldric lifted his hoof and pointed to a spot beyond the wall. Tommy and I shared an anxious glance and then slowly crawled out of the stable and up to the open door of the barn. From our position low to the ground the door seemed like a rectangle of space and stars cut into the side of the wall. It was like a portal to another world. And it was, in a way, it was a portal to aristocracy, marriage, theft, and by the looks of things, a very thin, mostly naked, old man with a long beard.

We watched him reach the house and shimmy open a window. He was wearing only a pair of y-fronts which were torn at the back revealing his pale buttocks and his long white beard reached the ground and dragged between his legs. He climbed in through the window and disappeared into the dark of the sleeping house.

'Who was that?'

'I think it was old Lord Witherbrick.'

'Why was he naked?'

'Dunno guv.'

We sat, crouched in the dark safety of the barn, and watched the window for Rochdale's ex-cat burglar to return. After a while the light in the room turned on and Perry appeared at the open window and looked at it quizzically. He lifted a hand and quietly shut it. Perry disappeared and the light in the room turned off.

'They don't know Witherbrick is in there,' said Tommy.

'Do you think we should do something?'

'Let's just see what happens.'

Suddenly there was a bang and the window shook. Old Witherbrick, not knowing the window had been shut, banged his face against it and fell out of sight. He got up and pulled the window open. It slid up quicker than I think he was expecting and he fell out and landed in a heap on the grass outside. It looked like the house had coughed up a tangled grey hairball. The light in the room turned on and Lord Witherbrick crouched against the wall and waited.

Perry appeared at the window and peered out of it, clearly looking to see what had made the noise and opened the window again. Witherbrick swung back something he was holding and wacked Perry hard in the forehead with it. CLONK! For a moment Perry just stood there, unmoved. He frowned as if working out a complicated riddle, seemed to come to a conclusion, closed his eyes, and fell backwards.

A window slid open on the second floor and Rochdale poked his head out. 'Witherbrick! What the hell are you doing? PERRY! Get out there and grab him!'

Witherbrick stepped back and looked up at Rochdale. He held the object he had hit Perry with up at Rochdale and skipped back and forth cackling wildly. The moon lit on his bare buttocks as he danced.

It was then, after I managed to drag my eyes from the hypnotising effect of those moonlit butt cheeks, that I saw what he had hit Perry with. It was the empty bottle of Shackleton's Whisky.

I stepped out of the shadow of the barn and Rochdale saw me.

'Richard! Stop him!'

Witherbrick span and faced me. He made his getaway and half ran, half skipped back up the lawn. I would never be able to catch him on foot. No one can run faster than an escaping mad man. There was only one way I was going to get him. It was clear that Baldric had come to the same conclusion. Tommy opened the stable door and Baldric stepped out and stood next to me. I turned and looked him in the eye. 'Are you sure about this?' I said.

Baldric nodded.

'He's getting away!' shouted Rochdale.

By this time Uncle Harry, Jones, William, and

Charleston, had all converged in the room that held the unconscious body of Perry. While Uncle Harry and the rest tended to Perry, Jones climbed out of the window and looked at me. He put his hand to his head and saluted. Baldric and I were the only hope. I saluted back. Baldric tried to do the same and nearly fell over. 'It's ok Baldric, you don't need to salute. Let's get him.'

The sun was coming up and as those first rays of solar luminescence shone over the horizon Baldric stepped forward and bowed to let me climb on to his back. I used his bowed knee as a step up and swung my leg over him. I wrapped my arms around his neck and said, 'Alright Baldric, this is your moment. Yah!'

Baldric reared up onto his back legs and neighed heroically. For a moment we must have looked like a gallant cowboy and his horse in the final scene of a great western, silhouetted by the sun and ready to save the day. And I wish I could end the story there. With some dignity. Immortalised forever in a silhouetted pose of glory. In reality I have never ridden a horse and Baldric, as previously suggested, isn't the smartest smarty in the smarty tube. He had over judged his rearing pose and we went tumbling backwards. It is uncomfortable to say the least to find yourself, still half drunk (which is why I say "uncomfortable" and not "In agonising pain due to being squished"), with a half mad horse writhing around on top of you trying to get back to its feet with the least amount of humiliation. I think he had it in mind to prove himself worthy under the watchful eyes of Rochdale.

When he did manage to get back on his feet I had suffered only a scraped thigh from the fall and Baldric had only scraped his pride. In the time it had taken to strike the pose, roll around dramatically on the floor and get back up again, Lord Witherbrick had managed to put some considerable distance between us.

Suddenly, from the darkness of the barn, Tommy appeared. He shot out of the darkness like an Olympic athlete running down-hill with the wind behind him. He leapt, from about six feet behind Baldric, and landed, legs splayed, on the horse's back with the style and ease of Clint Eastwood being directed by Guy Richie. I'm sure he's aware of how much this feat of elaborate equestrian straddling was showing me up, but still, the boy does have style.

Tommy kicked his legs and shouted 'Yah!' and Baldric galloped (galloped seems like the wrong word, it was more of an excited flounder) after Lord Witherbrick.

'Vagabond!' shouted Rochdale, assuming, I think, that Tommy was stealing the horse.

Tommy ignored Rochdale and removed a remote control (the kind you get with remote control cars) from his inside pocket. He extended the aerial (he turned out to be a deft horseman and was able to ride with no hands) and flicked a switch. From his trouser pocket he extracted a golf ball. I suddenly thought I had an idea as to what Tommy's plan might be.

Tommy and Baldric were gaining on Witherbrick but not by a lot. Although Baldric was making a valiant attempt at being the hero he was nevertheless stupid and clumsy. I mean, I have grown very fond of Baldric, but award winning horse he is not. If Tommy had chosen to ride an empty saddle he wouldn't have done much worse.

Tommy threw the golf ball high in the air and pressed a button on the remote. A flap fell open on the top of the ball and a small propeller popped out. Another flap opened at the back of the ball revealing a small exhaust pipe. The curious object hovered in the air for a moment as it sputtered and puffed into life. Tommy and Baldric were way ahead of the ball now and I wondered if I should head off on foot after them, there was a chance I could beat both him and the ball which was still currently motionless.

The propeller started spinning. It was making a chugging PUTT-PUTT sound. The ball seemed to find its bearings and then, like a hawk sighting prey, accelerated triumphantly toward old Lord Witherbrick and zoomed past Tommy and Baldric. In an instant it had gained on the old loon and clocked Lord Witherbrick on the back of the head. He was sent sprawling to the ground.

With Witherbrick now out of action Baldric and Tommy managed to catch up with him. Tommy dismounted Baldric and tied Witherbrick's hands together using his belt.

I was impressed. So much so that I clapped. 'Good work Tommy!' I hollered.

'How are you two acquainted!?' came the nerve shattering voice of Rochdale from the upstairs window. I turned to face him and shrugged noncommittally. 'Right! I'm coming down there! Nobody move!'

By the time Rochdale had erupted from the main entrance of the manor, Jones, William, Charleston, Uncle Harry, and I (presumably Natalie was still asleep somewhere, and Perry was no doubt still unconscious) were all standing around the mostly naked, and entirely defeated, Lord Witherbrick. Tommy and Baldric were standing next to each other, Tommy had his arms folded proudly. Baldric was panting happily and wagging his tail.

'You boy! How did you get out of the boot?'

Tommy glanced at me and then back at Rochdale. 'Boots can't hold me guv.' He said.

'What? What gibberish language is that?'

'It's cockney,' I said.

'Cockney! Ha! Tommy was born with a golden spoon in his mouth! Cockney my arse!'

Tommy rolled his eyes.

'I thought he was a happy go lucky street urchin. Like from a Charles Dickens novel,' I said. Though I did have my doubts.

'He's my dead wife's adopted sister's son.' (Get your head around that one!)

'Wouldn't that make him Natalie's cousin? It's no wonder you don't want him dating Tiffany.'

'There's no blood relation, Cyril's sister is adopted, as I just said. He's a step cousin at best. I don't want him dating Tiffany because he's a scoundrel and a thief!'

'I thought those were attributes you liked in a man?'

'I do, but not in a child!'

Tommy coughed into his hand to get our attention and then gave Rochdale the two finger salute.

'You see. Swearing at his elders, what kind of respect is that?'

'You've got to give him some credit though-'

'Let me tell you about our little hero here. Cyril's sister decided he wasn't worth the hassle and sent him to me to get straightened out. I immediately did the right thing and threw him out on the streets.'

'Chaps, I would like to remind you that I have just saved the day,' said Tommy, pointing at Lord Witherbrick, who was just beginning to stir.

'Ah yes, and by what magic did you achieve that?' Rochdale picked up the golf ball, which was quietly fizzing away on the ground near Witherbrick's head, and examined it. He raised an eyebrow and looked at me. 'Tell me Richard, how long have you and Tommy been in cahoots?'

'I don't know what you mean,' I said. And I didn't. What the hell does cahoots mean?

'I knew there was something dodgy about that little golf tournament of ours.'

'It wasn't really a tournament-'

'Shut up Richard. What's your game Tommy? And don't say chess.'

'You know me too well, guv-'

'And drop the whole cockney act while you're at it. What's your business helping Richard win a golf match and now catching Witherbrick? Are you trying to win a favour or something?'

I realised at this point that I had no idea what Tommy's real intentions for helping me were. At first I thought it was to get one over on Rochdale, but now I'm not so sure.

'What makes you think I have a reason? I saw Richard with Natalie in the village and thought, "Uh oh, I know what Rochdale's like. Probably going to kill the poor lad. I know! I think I'll help him out!" so that's what I did.'

Rochdale turned to me with what I think was a

sincere look in his eyes, 'Richard, pay no notice to the lad. You were never in any danger-'

'No *real* danger,' added Uncle Harry.

'I've come to like you actually.'

'Thanks,' I said.

While we were having this exciting conversation William and Charleston had dragged Witherbrick up to a nearby tree and leaned him against it. Harry had picked up the bottle and was holding it casually by his side. I frowned at it. 'Why was Witherbrick trying to steal an empty bottle?'

'Steal what?' said Rochdale, probably perplexed that I hadn't responded in kind to his warm sentiment.

'What did Lord Witherbrick want with an empty bottle?'

Rochdale frowned at me. 'It's priceless dear boy. Haven't you been paying attention?'

'But it's empty.'

'Jones can you explain things to Mr. Thicko over here while I get Lord Witherbrick inside for a bit of casual interrogation. And Tommy, you can get inside too, I'm not finished with you.'

And so off lurched the Roch to help manoeuvre the limp Witherbrick while Jones and I turned from the scene and tramped up to the house. Tommy followed. And so did Baldric.

Chapter Twenty-seven

By now Natalie had stirred. She was raising her head from the table as I entered with a man, a boy, and a horse.

'Hi,' she said, and then scrunched her face up at Tommy and Baldric. 'What are they doing here?'

I shrugged. It was a good question. Jones looked down at me with the same blank expression I had. He didn't know either. We looked at Baldric. He shrugged. Tommy sat down and answered for us. 'Rochdale sent us in. Baldric followed.'

'Daddy *wants* you in the house?' she said, curling her lip.

'Be nice. We're all friends now. I think.' I said, taking a seat next to her. 'Witherbrick tried to steal the empty Shackleton bottle. Jones, I believe you were going to fill me in on that one?' Jones slumped on a chair opposite us. Baldric trotted around the room admiring the portrait art on the walls.

Jones looked up at the ceiling, getting his thoughts together I imagine, and then looked down at me. His head looked heavy with a hangover. 'Think about it boy, no one on earth, apart from us, a Master Blender, and a Whisky expert, actually know what the drink tastes like. And besides, it's well known, or at least well-advertised, that the replica tastes identical to the original. It's the bottle that's worth the money-'

'Got it. That explains why no one minded drinking a priceless bottle of whisky. You can just fill it back up with the replica whisky and voila.'

'Yes, you got it. But to be honest we didn't steal it so we could sell it on. We stole it so we could drink it.'

Natalie joined in the convo. 'That's what Daddy's club does. They take what can't be bought. Not for profit. It's just a hobby.'

'And if we do happen upon a buyer with the right amount of cash we may sell it, we may not. If it will fund the next excursion then off it goes to the highest bidder. Otherwise it will get locked in the basement with the rest of the crap we've collected along the way.'

'I guess Witherbrick had other plans.'

'He's a con man. I've always said you can never trust a con man.'

'I thought you were all con men?'

'We are gentleman thieves. Scholarly scoundrels. We steal - plain and simple – we do not pull the fast one. We do not gain through deception. We do not CON! This is why your role is so important. The cat burglar is the purest member of our gang. He is true. He enters, he takes, and he leaves. It's the hardest crime to trace. A con always leaves a trail. Breaking and entry is criminal poetry. We are old men now, and most of us couldn't scale a wall, climb through a window, or any of the good old fun stuff. We gather blue prints. We locate the desirable. We enjoy the reward. But we try to do as little of the actual criminal stuff as possible. That's why we have you. And Witherbrick before you.'

'Hold on a minute, was Witherbrick a cat thief or a con man?'

'First of all, he wasn't a "cat thief". That would be a person who steals cats. He was a cat burglar. And he was both. He was a cat thief-'

'Burglar.' I corrected.

'Cat burglar, I mean, until he got bored and started craving something more illegally cerebral. Then he would seek the long con.'

'Oh. And by the way, I'm not a thief! I only stole for you so I could marry Natalie.' Natalie blushed.

Jones sat up slightly. 'That reminds me. Your wedding-'

'Oh yes?' I knew where this was going.

'I don't suppose you, how can I put it?'

'You don't suppose I have a good tailor in mind?'

'No it's not that, do you have a-'

'A top hat?'

'Err, no. Do you-'

'Have cold feet?'

'Let him finish,' said Natalie, seeing that I was making this unnecessarily difficult for him.

'Thank you Natalie. As I was saying. Many of my friends, and indeed I, have been married, yet-'

'You've never been a bridesmaid?'

'Yes! I mean no-'

'Jones, before you continue. I would like to ask you something.'

'What is it?'

'How are you at arranging stag-dos?'

His face lit up. 'I've never arranged one before, but I've thrown plenty of bashes, when you say arrange stag-dos? Are you asking me, what I mean to say is- listen,' he was in a bit of a flap. I didn't realise quite how much this meant to him. He stood up and walked around to my side of the table and sat down beside me. He put a hand on my shoulder and smiled. 'Are you asking me to be your best man?'

Now, let me just remind you dear reader of Jones's normal manner. He is a wooden man with little in the way of facial expressions. He is tall. He is mostly bald except for some neatly trimmed grey hairs around the sides. His brow is so solid it casts a shadow on his cheeks. He is a proper Englishmen and does not show any element of being human. Stiff as a board and as emotional as a depressed Easter Island Head.

I smiled. It was clear by the confused manner of his wrinkles that his eager grin was an entirely new expression. 'Yes.' I said.

He flung his arms wide and embraced me! 'Richard, dear fellow! I have come to admire and like you. It would be my honour to be your best man!'

'Ok.' I patted him on the back as he squeezed me. I really don't know what drives me to want to marry into this family and all its associates. I managed to turn my head enough to see Natalie. Even with the fresh corpse of a hangover looming over her she was the perfect image of beauty. Her hair was tangled in a way that would make most women seem tramp-like, but made her look dishevelled and ready for sex. But, as if to contradict that initial thought, her face was that of a photo-shopped dove. She smiled at me. It was a smile that would make the Mona Lisa reconsider her career options. Every time I see that smile I just want to hold her and kiss her, and never let her go. But right now I was holding Jones. And that's a lust dampener if ever there was one.

Jones let me go just as we heard the front door slam and footsteps echo through the entrance hall.

'Rochdale! I'm going to be best man!' shouted

Jones.

'Good for you Jonesy boy!'

That was a rare un-affected exchange between the two that somehow painted a picture of a long and old friendship. A friendship that had been bolted down and locked in the past in a safe made of etiquette and money.

Rochdale stomped past the door dragging Witherbrick behind him by the feet. We (all of us, including Baldric and Tommy) got up and followed.

Chapter Twenty-eight

We were in a room at the front of the house with one window that looked out at the long gravel driveway. Witherbrick was sat on a wooden chair. We all stood in front of him and watched him dribble on himself. Baldric stood in the hall with his head looking excitedly in to the room. The horse seemed very happy to be included.

I am going to take a liberty and assert that old Lord Witherbrick felt somewhat disorientated and unsure of his surroundings when he eventually came around. But how, you may be wondering, dare I assume to know what someone else is thinking? Well, I'll tell you how. When Lord Witherbrick came to he shouted, 'Pwaa, wrha-eaaargh, arghm I?' A statement, I'm sure you will agree, that gives us a firm insight into the baffled mind of this elderly man.

'Witherbrick! You buffoon! What do you think you are doing?' Witherbrick poked out a tongue and started to cackle. 'Tell me! What do you think you are playing at?'

'Rochdale you bloated dinosaur, what do you think I was doing? Stealin the trophy!'

'I know that, Witherbrick. But why were you stealing it in your underpants?!'

Witherbrick leaned forward and took on a serious demeanour. 'Well, don't you know, Rochdale? Don't you watch CSI?'

'No.'

'They can trace you. You know? From the fibres of

your clothes.'

Rochdale sighed. 'And what about the fibres from your beard?'

'How dare you!'

Jones leaned close to me and whispered in my ear. 'He's never accepted accusations that he has a beard. He's never believed it. It's the most curious thing. He gets offended if anyone even mentions the thing.'

'What?' I said, looking at Jones with a disbelieving furrow to my brow.

'I'll have you know I shave twice a day to avoid such things! I'm a professional.'

'You're insane. And also, you know damn well that I couldn't call the police-'

'They're called the CSI now-'

'No they're not. I couldn't call the police. What would I say? "Hello, one of my old gang stole this rare bottle of whisky I stole.".'

'You wouldn't!?'

'NO! Of course not! That's my point! I think you just like gallivanting around in your underpants! It's not right you know!'

Old Lord Witherbrick nodded in agreement. 'I do like to feel the air on my back.'

'I've decided to keep you as a pet. Any questions?' said Rochdale.

Witherbrick shook his head. This was a strange turn of events. His pet?

'There are prison cells in the tunnels that run under the Manor.' It was Jones whispering in my ear again (perhaps he heard my thoughts?), 'We've all been locked in there at some point over the years. Even Rochdale on one occasion. It's like a mutual prison in case one of us goes a bit off the rails. It happens from time to time, you know? Gives you time to think. The sentences are always short and we've found it makes the group stronger. Witherbrick holds the record for most time spent as a pet. He has one of his funny turns every two years or so. He'll be right as rain after a week or two in one of the cages.'

'That's crazy.'

'Yes, I suppose it is a bit.'

'Perry!' shouted Rochdale. Perry stooped in holding a bag of frozen peas to his head and awaited instruction. 'Could you prepare one of the cages for Lord Witherbrick? His usual one if you don't mind. And see that it's well stocked with cigars, whisky, and a selection of cheeses.' Perry nodded and wafted away. Rochdale turned to Witherbrick. 'I think you do this on purpose to get away from your wife.' The mad old Lord grinned a guilty grin and Rochdale sent him on his way. 'Do you need to be escorted or can I trust you to find your own way?'

'I know the way.'

'That's not what I asked.'

Rochdale let old Lord Witherbrick shuffle out of the room and take himself down to his cage, which suggests to me that this whole situation isn't as unusual as it first seemed. I mean it is unusual, it's very odd indeed, just not unusual for Rochdale and his ilk.

'TOMMY!' shouted the Roch.

Baldric trotted in. On top of him; Tommy. Rochdale looked at the horse with faint disregard and then up at the boy street urchin. Tommy smiled. 'Yes father?'

'I'm not your damn father!'

'My apologies. Yes, parental guardian?'

Rochdale clenched his fists and fumed silently. He spoke through gritted teeth. 'Fine. What is it you want from me?'

'A roof over my head and the freedom to talk to Tiffany whenever I want.'

'TOMMY! You can't have a relationship with my daughter! If I am you parental guardian, then she constitutes a sibling!'

Tommy jumped off the horse and landed like a silent monk. He stepped up to Rochdale and with each step came a new syllable. 'I – am – a – child.' Now he was standing chest to belly with Rochdale looking sternly up into his eyes. Rochdale looked sternly back. 'What is it you think I am going to do to her?'

'Incestuous things, my boy. You want to ruin my youngest daughter!'

'Rochdale! I AM A CHILD! I don't know *how* to ruin your daughter! I just want to play tag with her. Or maybe play computer games together! Or go to the park and play on the swings! You misjudge me, man, I am too young to be a bloody sex pest!'

A child, even if it was Tommy, saying "sex pest" with such gusto put us all on the back foot. He was right of course. Tommy is just a child. A sneaky genius child.

Rochdale exhaled slowly. He narrowed his eyes at Tommy and looked over at me. 'What do you think?'

'Me?' I said. Rochdale waited but did not reply. 'Well, actually, not only do I think you should let him live here, I also think he would be an asset to the team.'

'Richard! Some things should not be spoken about around the uninitiated!'

'He knows all about it. He kind of told me about it

before I even knew I was being tested.'

'He could be right.' It was Jones. He was holding the flying golf ball and inspecting it carefully. 'Tell me, Tommy, where did you get this contraption?'

'I made it. Along with many other awesome gadgets.'

Jones turned to Rochdale, 'It's a modern world out there old man. The old way we do things is becoming harder and harder. Maybe a tech guy would be a needed addition to the group.'

Rochdale looked Tommy up and down. 'Do you know what we're talking about young lad?'

Tommy rolled his eyes and leant against Baldric. 'You lot, now including Richard, are members of an elite team of thieves, headed by yourself, Rochdale. Uncle Harry is the muscle. William and Charleston, as well as being avid explorers, are essentially the brains behind the operation, they find the blueprints and plan the robbery etc. Natalie is the pretty girl – often used as a decoy – and Jones is simply a man of reason. He enjoys the spoils and he has many contacts that help ease the whole process; Judges, chiefs of police, influential members of parliament etc. And Richard is your common cat burglar. Old Witherbrick was the cat burglar but is now more of an aging demented pet that no one wants to put down. You are probably going to keep him close in case you one day need a patsy. And also, I can do this.'

'Do what?' said Rochdale, (who looked admittedly impressed by Tommy's insight).

Tommy pulled his iPad out of his shoulder bag and with some swift finger movements brought up the CCTV of the room we were in. He showed us.

'Is that us?' said Rochdale, waving a hand to see if it was live. The image on the screen was taken from above his right shoulder. 'You have access to my CCTV?'

'Yes, and that's not all,' said Tommy.

With a few more swift movements of his fingers the iPad did something astonishing. He pressed a button and the sound of an engine firing up blasted in from the driveway outside. It was Rochdale's car. The headlights came on and the engine revved. We all stared out of the window.

'Perry!? Is that you out there?' shouted Rochdale.

'It's me,' said Tommy. 'I have been making small adjustments to your car for some time now. You locking me in the boot yesterday gave me the time I needed to finish my improvements.'

Using the iPad as a control Tommy slid his thumb up the right side of the screen. The virtual lever he was manipulating moved the car forward. We all watched as Rochdale's beloved Rolls Royce drove into view. And then, using the iPad just like a steering wheel, turning it in his hand, the car turned and faced us. The headlights beamed into the room casting a grid of shadows on us from the panelled windows.

'Hold on now, what's the meaning of this Tommy?'

'Just a demonstration.'

Tommy pushed the virtual lever and the car roared forward and hurtled towards us. There was not enough time to run. I instinctively (regardless of how ineffective this would actually be had the car hit) held up my arms to protect myself from the impact. Rochdale and the others did the same. Tommy turned the iPad sharply to the left and the Rolls Royce cornered and skidded past the window sending a shower of gravel at us. A few panels smashed but we were all left unharmed. Tommy was still turning the car to its left and it slowly came back into view and stopped in front of the window. Tommy flicked a virtual switch and the headlights turned off and the engine died.

'Remarkable,' said Rochdale. 'What else can you do?'

'I am capable of remarkable technological feats. All of which will remain a secret unless I am made a fully-fledged member of your little group. There will be no restrictions on hanging out with Tiffany, and I will promise to never have romantic feelings towards her.' (This, I believe, was a lie) Rochdale looked at Jones. 'And one more thing,' said Tommy, 'you apologise to Baldric for beating him up.'

Rochdale's shoulders sagged. 'You're making the assumption that you are in a position to barter with me.'

Tommy flicked a switch on his iPad and the Rolls Royce roared back into life. It lurched forward. In its path, about a hundred yards away, was a rather large oak tree.

'Ok! Stop! Fine, you can join us.' Tommy stopped the car. 'There are conditions though. We have full access to any gadget you make. You never so much as touch Tiffany! But you can hang out with her. And finally, Richard-' he turned to me.

'Me?'

'You have to take full responsibility for this dangerous and insane child! Anything he does wrong is equally your fault!'

Tommy looked at me and smiled like a puppy.

'I think I should discuss this with Natalie.'

'I'm out here,' came her voice from the hall. 'I couldn't get past Baldric. Daddy, Richard and I are not adopting Tommy.'

'I'll be good,' promised the creepy, secretly posh, street urchin.

'You don't have to adopt him. Just keep an eye on him.'

'I don't mind doing that,' I said.

'I'll be no trouble, I promise,' said Tommy.

Natalie was silent for a moment. 'He *is* trouble Richard.'

I had just realised the child had grown on me and the thought of being a partial guardian to the lad appealed to me. Or technically, what I really liked the sound of was to have him looking out for me. He's done a fine job of it so far. I'll pretend to be his guardian, when really he's being mine. Not that I would admit that to anyone of course.

'Natalie, I'll take full responsibility for him. And you won't even notice I'm doing it. He's self-contained really. It will be like having a pet that's better at doing stuff than you are.'

'Better than me at what?!'

'No, I meant you as in "me", just generally handy to have around. Inventing stuff and being a genius mastermind, but in our favour. That kind of thing.'

'Richard. I am going to bed. You decide what we are doing. You can tell me about it in the morning. But, I warn you, if you decide to take him on, I am not getting involved. And if he becomes a problem then we are handing him straight back over to Daddy for him to do as he pleases with him. Agreed?' Natalie started to walk off.

'Agreed. Natalie?'

She stopped walking. 'Yes?'

'I've decided to keep him!'

She sighed. 'Fantastic. Wonderful news. Goodnight Richard.'

I turned to Tommy. 'You can be the ring bearer at the wedding!'

'Happy days!' said Tommy.

Epilogue

Rochdale begrudgingly agreed to give Baldric a bigger stable and he even let me put a television set in there for the mad horse to watch.

Baldric loved the television. He loves a bit of Red Dwarf but his favourite show is Only Fools and Horses. Although he was disappointed in the sitcom at first. He thought it was going to be about stupid humans and smart horses. But the disappointed was soon replaced with mirth as the show progressed. (Baldric has a truly infectious laugh. We were watching that bit when Del Boy falls through the bar and Baldric bust into hysterics. His eyes were closed, his shoulder were shuddering, and his neighs were like staccato sneezes. If you've never seen a horse laugh I urge you to go out and find a horse to amuse. It will be well worth the effort). Although there are no horses in Only Fools and Horses, Baldric has decided that Trigger is in fact a horse (what with that face and that name) and he seems to relate to his character.

I gave Baldric the box set of 24 and he watched it for 8 days straight with no sleep. When it was done Baldric's personality had morphed into that of Jack Bauer. He was very serious and suspicious of everything. He walked around like he had singlehandedly saved mankind. Baldric had become a heartless hard-ass. I knew he would snap out of it though (and he did after a few days) the same thing happened to me when I watched the bloody show.

The reason I'm banging on about Baldric's

television watching is because it was the thing that finally brought Baldric and Rochdale together. I let Baldric watch an episode of The X-Files. That poor horse. It terrified him. He had nightmares for days. He was convinced his stable was haunted and told me (in his own horsey way) that aliens had landed in the grounds of the manor. After the third day of having a very scared horse around the place, avoiding his stable and looking suspiciously around the grounds (poking his head in to bushes, checking under the cars, suddenly getting spooked and running into the house etc.) Rochdale asked me what was up with him. I told him it was all down to a single episode of The X-Files and Rochdale's face turned white.

It turned out that Rochdale was terrified of the show. He'd watched an episode of it in the mid-nineties and didn't stop having nightmares well into the new millennium. A resolute, almost charitable, look came over him and he marched away from me, out of the house, and down to the stables. When I went down to see what was going on I found Baldric and Rochdale in an emotional embrace. This common fear of a cult TV show had brought them together. Rochdale stayed in the stable with Baldric that night and has been visiting him regularly since.

Tommy was given his old room back. His room was in the attic and is essentially a self-contained flat. He had his own bathroom and the room is in three sections. One section has his bed in it, the second is done up like a little lounge with a TV and couch, and the other section had been turned into a kind of workshop/laboratory. I was kind of jealous at first (all

Natalie and I had was a room with an en-suit bathroom). But he was happy up there and I visit him often and we watch films together. He shows me his new inventions and gadgets. He is a truly remarkable boy. My favourite invention of his was a block of cheese that was shaped like a chocolate bar. That's not really an invention, I know, but there's just something very satisfying about snapping off a square of cheese. He also invented an electric shaver that was shaped like a beard. The idea being that you could shave your whole face with one single movement. I tried it and it nearly took my face clean off.

Natalie's warming to him but still distrusts him. He made her an electric hair brush as a peace offering. She gave in and accepted it, building that first small bridge to an eventual bond, but she never used the brush. To be honest we're both a bit afraid of it. It looks like a torture device and we're not exactly sure what it does. After the incident with the electric shaver we've decided it's best to never find out.

Tommy has realised, I think, that home products are not his forte and has since stuck mostly to inventing and improving surveillance equipment, weapons, and gadgets for sabotage and theft.

Rochdale and I have the same relationship we've always had. I fear him and he torments me. But at the same time he is enormously protective over me and seems to hold me in high regard.

Witherbrick was eventually let out of his cage and sent back home. The madness seemed to have seeped out of him and he apologised for his actions. Jones gave him about 8 months before the lunacy crept back into his deranged old mind.

After the departure of Witherbrick the others went back to their own mansions and manors. All who was left in the house was myself, Natalie, Tommy, Rochdale, Perry, Tiffany, and the horses. It was nice. We were like a little malfunctioning but content family. As far as anyone can tell Tommy has indeed kept his hands off Tiffany. Occasionally they go to the cinema together, or the penny arcade in town, but they just seem to be very good friends. But one suspects a well-kept secret romance is afoot.

Afterward

A few days before the wedding a mysterious envelope appeared in my room. Perry had placed it on the side table next to the bed. I walked over to it and picked it up. The envelope was made of fine black card. Written on the front, in startling white ink, was my name:

Richard

I opened the envelope and inside was a plain black card. I extracted it. On it was a very short message. It said, in hand written white ink:

The Game has started
A car is waiting for you outside
Bring slippers

The stag do had begun and it would turn out to be one of the most intense and harrowing few days of my life.

THE END...

*****

Thank you for reading. If you made it this far I suspect you need a drink, but before you head out into the wild, and if you enjoyed it, please help get the word out by leaving a review at the book's Amazon page (or even on Goodreads if you happen to be a member).

For more words from this author you can check out his blog at the address below or harass him on Twitter @AndyChapWriter

http://andychapwriter.wordpress.com